Fatal Contracts

Shocking Short Stories with a Sting in the Tale

David R Tollafield

Cover by Petya Tsankova with artists
Timon Studler & Brandi Redd

Published by Busypencilcase
Communications

'Contracts'

There are many forms of contracts but
officially it is an agreement between two
private parties, creating mutual legal
obligations. A contract can be either oral
or written.

David R Tollafield

EXTRACT

The older woman's face looked like leather, with deep flaccid creases. Her teeth were poor, her nose small and stubby and her hair thin and grey. Alison thought she must be a hundred and fifty! Close by a candle burned with two joss sticks supported in tall thin glass holders. The scent was strong, if not overpowering. It seemed different to the joss sticks she had used when visiting friends as a teenager. They had been all the rage then.

Ying Ma turned the cards over. The candle flickered. There was no wind but the candle seemed to shift of its own accord. The light altered so darkness transcended the room. Alison thought this was all an act.

The older woman reacted and spoke rapidly.

'What's she saying?' Alison asked the younger woman.

'I dunno, she upset about somfin!'

The old soothsayer rocked back and forwards then leaned forward and grabbed Alison's hand. The cards lying on the table had previously depicted individual scenes of The Magician, The High Priestess, The Empress, The Lovers, Wheel of Fortune, Justice and The Hangman, but now skeletal Death, riding a horse with a scythe in his left hand, replaced each. On the top of the card known as Death, 'numeral XIII' appeared within a scroll.

'What does this mean?' not liking the image very much. Alison felt a shiver go up to her spine, despite the confined space and the heat of the day.

A Strange Affair

David R Tollafield

CONTENTS

STICKY CONTRACTS 1

OBSESSION 16

THE SALESMAN 31

THE WITHERED HAND 54

THE PISCARRO CONTRACT 77

BRODIE'S DECEPTION 105

OPERATION KALAVRYTA 130

A STRANGE AFFAIR 152

ACKNOWLEDGMENTS 173

ABOUT THE AUTHOR 175

STICKY CONTRACTS

The drab location beneath London Bridge Station had
been begging for money and development, so it was
converted into the current tourist attraction: The London
Dungeon. It always had long queues. As he moved
forwards, he stumbled. At last, the ticket booth window
was in sight. The attendant peered at him. She could see
he had bloodshot eyes. His skin was bad, and he had a
crusty red rash around his nose. Taking in the grim
features of this lanky, longhaired man, she shuddered.
'You don't look as though you should be here. You
drunk or something?' she asked, with the frustration
anyone would have given the size of the queue which
wound down Tooley Street.

'... just give me a ticket,' Bloodshot Eyes said.

'And don't think you're getting in, mate. You're high
as a kite.'

'Oi, you, move on. Some of us want to get a look in
before the bloody place shuts.'

Those closest in the queue soon voiced their impatience. The sun beat down and water bottles were emptying quickly. Realising his colleague needed help, one of the street ushers moved in.

'Come on, mate. You heard the lady. You're not getting in today. Sober up, okay? And piss off.'

Bloodshot Eyes put his hand on the wooden sill of the ticket office to steady himself. Something in his hand compressed like a sandwich against the counter. He snatched the item away, looked at the yellow outer casing, cursed and pushed himself off. He staggered onto the street, bumping into a number of people as he tried to focus.

'What's going on, Sam?' a teenager with flame-red hair asked her friend. The two girls had been waiting patiently, taking in the crowd chattering away in foreign tongues.

'Reckon some git's tried to get in and he's two parts gone to the wind!'

Becky was the taller and slimmer of the two. She had persuaded Sam to break off from studying just once and come and enjoy herself. Playing truant from school was not something Sam would usually entertain.

A sudden mass of laughter arose and Becky joined in. Sam could not see what was funny and scowled.

'Come on, Sam. You've got to lighten up.'

'Yeah, well, I'm not sure this is my thing. It better not be scary.'

'You'll be fine,' her friend assured her.

The usher moved down. His sallow cheeks were accentuated with dark makeup and gave him the obscene appearance of a ghoul. His hair, a wig, was ludicrously dishevelled and hung over his shoulders, tucked under a black top hat so the dark hair stuck out. His jacket had tails and seemed short at the sleeves. His trousers had black stripes reminding Becky of 'Beetlejuice', a film she had once seen.

'Keep moving and keep to the side, we have lovely tourists who don't want to have to walk in the street now.' And tourists indeed had to walk in the road as the pavement was narrow and the location wholly unsuitable given the constant spill of passengers emerging from the nearby underground and mainline station. With the River Thames nearby, Tower Bridge sparkled, painted freshly in blue, and the Tower of London was also visible. This part of London, just south of the river, was a hive of humanity eager to savour the sights of the capital city of England.

While the usher made his way down one side, a woman wearing a white blouse, dark dress and a dirt-stained apron completed the impression that this was an unhygienic experience in the making.

Sam shuddered as she took in the usher's respective garb. 'I'm sure I'm not going to like this place.'

'You'll be just fine,' Becky replied, trying to hide her frustration and wondering whether her oversized friend should really have come. In fact, Sam was her last choice as two other friends had shown less willingness. Sam's mother had made it all happen.

'Becky, for heaven's sake, Sam needs to get out a bit and away from all the studying. It'll do her good.'

'You don't mind her skipping school, Mrs Parsons?'

'I won't tell if you won't, but she's been a bit down and we are fighting to get her diabetes under control. She's not losing any weight and Chris and I are frantic.' Becky nodded, she really didn't need all this information.

As the girls moved forwards slowly alongside the brick-coloured building, the traffic buzzed past noisily. Becky wondered what she had taken on. A sickly girl and one who might chicken out. She'd been dying to visit the dungeons for some time but the absolute truth was that some of her mates had egged her on telling her she's got to go. 'Show the boys you're not scared. That'll impress them.'

Finally at the desk, the ticket lady looked at them to check that they were over 12 years old. She took in the girls, processing the information quickly.

'How many?' the woman barked.

'Two tickets, please,' Beck answered politely, grabbing the sill to lean closer. She pulled away quickly and looked at her hand. 'Yuck!'

'Have you got a paper towel or something?' she asked.

'Use the bathroom like everyone else, now move on.'

'She's not very friendly,' Sam said.

'No, you're right there. She could do with going to people management classes. Sam, I won't be a minute,' and she disappeared before Sam could complain she was abandoned.

The gaseous smell of old London sewers was artificially pumped into the museum. Actors supported the odd animatronic models, adding to the scary scenes spread around haphazardly. 'This is so cool, innit?' Becky screeched as she felt the wind blow onto their faces. A body suddenly thrust itself into the eerie black atmosphere suspended by a safety cable.

'I dunno, it's pretty scary, not sure this was a good idea!' Sam coughed. 'This smoke isn't good for my asthma.'

'I thought you had diabetes?'

'Yeah, and asthma, plus I've got to watch my allergies,' Sam replied

'Come on, don't be such a plebbo,' Becky retorted, with a new word she had just picked up. Sam would have been more at home in the Science Museum in

South Kensington rather than the dungeons. She was already regretting it. How could her mother have agreed? They stood by a scene where rocks clunked onto a thick wooden board, which wobbled across the chest of a man. He appeared emaciated and was tethered to the ground in chains so he could not move. This was a depiction of cruelty from the Middle Ages. The lifelike model's head was extended back and turned to the side so the visitors could see the contorted face. The horror and pain of the act emanated in one unforgettable picture of torment. Each rock added to the existing weight designed to crack ribs. The visceral organs sustaining life were crushing his life and no doubt haemorrhaging as the damage continued. "This is so great,' Becky shrieked.

The citizens of London were being sentenced to death in so many gory ways, bent impossibly in different directions so the muscles and bones cracked and joints popped out of sockets. 'It doesn't leave much to the imagination, does it?' Becky delighted in this masochistic self-imposed scaremongering.

'And you like this stuff?' Sam asked, coughing a little more. As the girls moved forward from one exhibit to the next, the Tooley Street queue joined them. Doubtless each person had been accosted by the curt tones of the ticket women who had the patience of a hound wanting supper. Out of prominent view a small notice appeared to be the only disclaimer visible.

ALL YE WHO ENTER BEWARE, FOR
GHOSTIES AND GHOULIES ARE ABOUT
TO GIVE YOU FRIGHT. ANYONE WITH
MEDICAL CONDITIONS, OR THOSE WHO
ARE PREGNANT OR OF NERVOUS
DISPOSITION SHOULD SEEK ADVICE OR
MEDICAL ATTENTION. THE
MANAGEMENT CAN TAKE NO

RESPONSIBILITY. YOU ENTER AT YOUR
OWN RISK.

It would be fair to say that neither girl had seen the sign
especially as it was in black with faded white writing. It
was far from obvious. Being placed out of direct sight
did not help either. 'Yuck, this is so gross, Becky.
You're weird if you ask me!' The corridors replicated
the old Bethlem 'mental' hospital, with its dark
walkways. Strobe lights and echoed noises created
imposing sounds which amplified the effect. Screams
from inmates in the cells where they had been
committed for the most elementary of transgressions
offered the visitor an idea of their sorrowful plight. A
tall figure crossed their path holding a long pole.
Perched on one end was a sharp-looking curved blade.
He stood with a dark hood covering his long face. Any
details were lost behind the cavernous covering but his
long spindly fingers beckoned from his equally
longhand, pointing at the girls. Sam started to cough
again and brought out a blue inhaler. She took two puffs
as Becky was looking at the figure. Becky touched the
pole, sliding her hand up the length but was unable to
reach the blade. She sniffed her hand after withdrawing
from the inspection. 'Interesting. I can smell a definite
smell.'

'I'm surprised you can make anything out here given
the conflicting aromas.' Sam might have appeared a
wimp but she was knowledgeable and well-read. She
knew a fair amount about London's asylum but as she
stared at the tall figure she said, 'You know who that is
don't you?'

'A bloody tall man in black if you ask me.'

'No silly, that's the Grim Reaper.'

'What's that then?' Becky asked. Becky was not the
brightest pupil, primarily as she focused on ethereal
aspects of life which extended to her beauty and boys!

'He was a mythical figure from the 14th century in Europe which probably came about from the effects of the Black Death. You know that plague that happened and killed thousands.'

'What's with the pole then?'

'That's a scythe and was an implement used to harvest crops. So in some ways it's a euphemism, no, maybe a metaphor for cutting life out!'

'You really are a geek, Sam, do you know that?'

Sam smiled at her pretentious friend with her golden hair and smooth skin. Only her skin shimmered red in the artificial light. The girls moved on. Becky had gone quiet. Sam thought she was absorbing the lesson just offered. The Grim Reaper was a bit of a sinister character. Sam was starting to enjoy herself a little more.

Entering a very dark room, Becky looked up. A figure appeared, along with a flickering aura of light. This was no animatronic or model as it hovered fluidly. Taller than the Reaper had been at seven foot, the figure leaned down over Becky. Sam was utterly unaware but she felt the hairs on her arm stand up. The air went cool and she put this down to the intelligent temperature controls between the various rooms and exhibits. Becky crashed to the cold stone floor in slow motion. She would not get up again.

Red light appeared, then golden light and the bars of prisons appeared, with more grisly unhygienic faces looking out, illuminated for effect. Amidst the screams, it would take some time before anyone realised that Becky needed medical care. Sam's screams, though, had been the loudest.

On reaching the hospital, Becky was pronounced dead. The junior doctor on duty at Guy's Hospital signed the death certificate – '*idiopathic stroke*'. The idiopathic bit suggested the doctor didn't know entirely what had caused it, and a coroner was required. The hearing was intended to be routine. The need for an inquest concerning a young girl dying in a public location with any vague diagnosis was necessary by law. Mrs and Mrs Robbins, Becky's parents, could not request an autopsy, but the coroner had appreciated the junior doctor's consultant making the suggestion that one would be of value. Not only that, the consultant had a daughter and would understand the Robbins' utter loss and disbelief at their daughter's sudden death.

Sitting in the room where the inquest was being held by the coroner, the properly interested people attending – or PIPs as they were known – included the parents, the pathologist and a man called Simon Hepford for the company that owned and managed the Tooley Street museum. Hepford sat nervously at the back with a smaller man who would turn out to be his solicitor.

The Robbinses also had a solicitor.

On hearing of the death of their daughter and only child, they were shocked, followed by guilt at not having been there. They were distressed, confused, then disconsolate, with Becky's mother becoming depressed. The anger set in then, seeking blame.

'Why did Becky have to die? Surely that fat girl should have died. She was the one with all the medical problems.' Mrs Robbins spoke out as extended family had gathered in their sitting room after Becky's untimely demise.

'I want to know who was responsible for her death,' her husband said, anger in his voice.

'Look Jeff, you're not going to know anything until the coroner has more details and you must be alive to the fact that there may be no reason. Young people often die without any cause being found,' George Graham, the solicitor acting for the Robbinses said.

'That grease pit of a museum is badly run. They're negligent and that sign was not worth the...' He paused and spat out, 'Paper!'

'I agree, the notice does constitute a contract between the company and benefactor but this is a woolly area in law.'

The Parsons, Sam's parents, attended the hearing as well, but Sam was too upset. Coming to terms with her friend's death was a big deal. Even the police had interviewed her. All she could say was that it had been very noisy and the lighting made it difficult to see in the dark.

The pathologist who worked for the Home Office took the stand. The room was adorned as a court but perhaps not quite as majestic as some. The coroner was legally trained, rather than being medically qualified, and was dressed in a dark suit and red tie. Mr Fergus Timmins was highly experienced. Timmins had provided an outline of the purpose of the hearing and would try to convey as much sensitivity as possible over the unfortunate young woman's death. There would be no need for a jury as this was a matter of dealing with the facts as they appeared. He of course had had sight of the pathologist's report already, but wanted to explore some of the lesser-known details, as well as ask Mr Hepford a few questions.

'Please Dr Turner, explain your findings to assist this inquest into the untimely death of Miss Rebecca Robbins.'

Muriel, Becky's mother sobbed loudly in her seat, and Timmins lifted his head to see who it was. Jeff put his arm around his wife. Directing his attention back to Turner, Timmins continued.

'Could you please start by providing a summary of your report?'

Turner started by presenting Becky's results in the usual manner. These amounted to a vocabulary that few might understand and hardly seemed remotely related to the life of someone so young and healthy.

'Miss Rebecca Robbins was a 15.9-year-old Caucasian female who lived with her parents and was admitted to Guy's Hospital on the 28th May and pronounced dead on arrival. She was referred by Dr Mithelian, Consultant Physician as he did not feel the preemptory cause of death was a stroke.'

Twenty-five minutes later, Timmins put his own pen down as Turner concluded.

'So you feel that there were some blisters around the skin region of the nose and lips and that her larynx was swollen consistent with anaphylactic shock,' said Timmins. He was trying to convert the doctor's medical explanation for easier understanding by his audience.

Turner continued. 'As you are aware, this is the most toxic of all the immune responses but in a girl of this age there is usually not only a trigger but a reason that this has occurred. Such sensitivity would normally take place initially with a mild response. From samples of tissue in the respiratory system there appear to have been a massive cellular change. This would involve the mucosa of the bronchi…'

'That's the lining of the branches of the airways within the lungs isn't it?'

'Yes, histology shows inflammatory eosinophilia, and epithelial sloughing. Serum concentrations of mast cell tryptase was noted on necropsy. The IgE was notable but the allergen appears to be glue.'

'And what evidence is there for this, Dr Turner?' Timmins said, sounding equally surprised. 'Well, two features seem to stand out. There were blisters around the thenar eminence...'

'You mean the skin between the thumb and hand?'

Turner seemed oblivious to the use of medical terminology, and intended as he always did to stick to the facts. Facts told the story and you could not soften the blow. He also was a bit dismissive because a legal person was taking court and not an experienced medic.

'Yes, of course. Whether the deceased rubbed her face is unclear but consistent with transmitting the allergen to that part of her body.'

'So Dr Turner, what you are suggesting is that Rebecca Robbins acquired glue and was responsible for transmitting what in her case was poison to her system, and thus suffered a massive inflammatory response?'

Dr Turner was not one who smiled often but Timmins had understood the situation clearly and maybe was not such an uninformed idiot as he had thought. As Turner confirmed Timmins's interpretation as accurate, the coroner understood the reason for the smile. He scribbled on his pad – *check police report.*

Jeff Robbins took the stand.

'Now Mr Robbins, I know this is very difficult, but from Dr Turner's findings you understand your daughter had a chemical reaction. We know the factor that set off a series of severe reactions, which as Dr Turner has intimated, is unusual without a trigger. That is clearly something that sets off the reaction. But, and here's the rub if you like, was there anything in Rebecca's history that suggested she had a prior sensitivity to any substance?'

'No sir, and I know what you're thinking, was she a glue sniffer, and Muriel and I know for a fact she would never touch drugs or anything like that. Our girl...' he sniffed and brought out a clean handkerchief and blew his nose, then continued... 'was particular about her appearance and skin and she knew about glue and what it could do. We are baffled by the suggestion that there was glue on her fingers.'

Jeff Robbins was allowed to return to his wife. 'I'm not calling Rebecca's friend, but from notes taken by the police, Miss Parsons mentioned that her friend left for the toilet soon after entering the museum. We have not ascertained why but there is some suggestion that after placing her hands on the ticket counter she may have accidentally made contact with something. Mr Hepford, please step up and provide your account.'

Simon Hepford was tall and somewhat rounded with thinning fair hair and a non-descript moustache that Timmins regarded as 'bum fluff'. His chin dimple seemed out of place and he had noticeably coloured cheeks. If Hepford could have spoken his mind he would have said he was shitting himself. His stomach was all over the place and he had been to the loo five times already. He was petrified this would cost him his job. Despite all the soothing comments made by Hepford's solicitor, who in fact represented the company rather than Hepford, Simon Hepford was a bag of nerves.

'Just stick to the facts. Don't get angry or try to defend any action,' Jerry Marsden, legal counsel, had advised. 'Sound sympathetic, as your museum just had a fatal accident and we don't yet know why. Okay – have you got that?'

'Now Mr Hepford, can you tell us what was found on the counter of the ticket office?'

'Er, yes sir, we found a sticky substance which proved quite difficult to remove.'

'How do you think that substance came to be there, Mr Hepford?'

'Well sir, we don't know. The evening cleaning team found it and thought it unusual because it smelled odd.'

'Is it possible someone put it there? As it was an adhesive, is it likely that your maintenance team would have used it?'

'I don't know. I leave that up to them.' Thinking he might have been rude he said, 'Sorry, what I meant to say was that I'm not qualified to say as my maintenance team takes care of all these things.'

'Yes, I understand...'

'Well I think we have heard from everyone now and so we can conclude that Rebecca was in the wrong place at the wrong time and had a contact sensitivity that caused her to have a massive anaphylactic response. We have heard the evidence from Dr Turner and it is clear this is rare. The toxicology, as Dr Turner mentioned in his report, was negative to any drugs so we can exclude ingested sources or drug abuse. My findings are that we have a death caused by misadventure and circumstances beyond anyone's control. I want to thank everyone who has assisted in this most unfortunate event and to offer my condolences to the parents of Rebecca.'

Timmins left the room, but not before Jeff Robbins had shouted out, 'What about negligence? What about my daughter's rights? The museum was responsible for her death.' He stabbed his fingers and raged at Simon Hepford who shrank back and wanted to visit the toilet yet again.

There was never an easy way to conclude such an upsetting hearing and he was indeed remorseful at not having a better verdict.

Hepford broke down at home, and his wife tried to console him. 'Jean, I couldn't say but maintenance bodged a repair on that bloody figure of the Grim Reaper. They had a young recruit on that day and he piled glue all over the pole. He told me. You hear! He told me, and I just let it rest. I said we could wait until the main man got back...'

Bloodshot Eyes slumped against the grimy wall of an alley. His moth-eaten jacket lay open and his shirt and jumper rode up, exposing his pink belly. The plastic bag covered his face and he breathed in heavily. His legs spread out as the effects of the toluene-based chemical took over. He groaned as a tall shadow appeared over the semi-recumbent body propped up in the tunnel. There was no-one else around. The figure appeared with a flickering aura of light, and the body moved fluidly as if hovering. Taller than the model of the Grim Reaper had been, the figure leaned down over Bloodshot Eyes. All life disappeared as his heart muscles ceased to work. The toxicity had finally done its job. No one would be suspicious as 'death' claimed another victim.

Author's Note

I confess that as a 21-year-old student I loved wax museums and in 1978, I took my girlfriend to the London Dungeon that I described. Animatronics had not been developed at the time of our visit but the man with rocks across his torso was one of those abiding memories, as were the smells. Simon Hepford is an imaginary character and to the best of my knowledge no one ever died, and the museum's staff were not as depicted. Madame Tussauds owns the London Dungeon, which relocated to the Queen's Walk, South Bank in 2013 and there is no intended slight on their management. Doubtless the move from Tooley Street was deemed safer with the mounting congestion around London Bridge station. Today, tickets can be bought on line making life easier, but the packed queues were another of my memories as I had to frequent the area as part of my career.

The story is wholly fictional. Although in the eighties glue sniffing was rampant and deadly, this is less prevalent now. As Dr Turner pointed out, it is unusual to go from a chemical reaction to full-blown anaphylactic shock at the first exposure. Given swift medical care, new cases survive with treatment. Although London Bridge Hospital was closer, I selected Guy's Hospital.

The mysterious bringer of death has not disappeared and will appear in a later story so read on to find out which chapter the strange apparition will appear in again.

OBSESSION

Love is a feeling; marriage is a contract,
relationships are work.

Frank had settled in his favourite chair. It was moth-eaten in appearance but the heavy wear was due to sitting for long periods. The armchair had a familiar patina where his hand had discoloured the fabric over time. It was early morning. Having finished breakfast, he digested the morning's newspaper cover to cover. As was his fashion he commenced at the breakfast table then retired to the living room, where he would take a second cup of tea. As his tea had not been delivered, his wife's lack of attention unsettled him. The tea was necessary and allowed him to feel entirely at home. Frank was a man who liked routine. He was engrossed in a local story, his old magnifying glass poised across the pages in a posture characterised by Arthur Conan Doyle's Sherlock Holmes. He believed that it was rare for his county to be mentioned in the tabloids he surmised as his eyes arrested on one particular piece.

> Two youths were arrested by police today,
> having stolen an Impreza from a
> supermarket car park. They had driven to a
> local school where they smashed through a
> new fence and tore up the playing fields. No
> one was hurt. Both boys aged14 who could
> not be named due to being underage, will
> appear before a juvenile court on Thursday.
> School Head Mr Todd Finlay said, 'If this
> had happened during the day, somebody
> could have been killed.

Frank hated to be disturbed when reading, which included being irritated by his wife standing at the window and peering out.

'I think you should come away from the window, dear. It's rude to stare!'

Philippa turned to her husband. 'It's the woman over the road, that's the third delivery she's had this week.'

'Yes it's all very well, but it's none of our business.' He wanted to tell his wife about the youths but she interrupted and said,

'Oh look, he's coming here!'

The postman knocked holding a small box in his hands. His dreadlocks were tucked under his cap. His cheery smile greeted Philippa as she opened the door.

'Oh, you're new?' taking in the dreadlocks. Philippa had seen very few West Indian men, and then only on the TV.

'Can I help?' she interjected before he had a chance to speak.

'Tanks, would you be able to take this in for number 34 please? Oh, and please sign here.'

Philippa took the odd-looking machine in her hands. It looked a bit like a large mobile phone, as it had a similar screen.

'Oh, hang on, I need my glasses,' and left the man at the door while she went in to find her reading specs. The postman watched her disappear back into the cottage and stood whistling his favourite tune, unfazed, in the time it took Phillipa to return. 'There we are, dear, let me look,' she said, her reading glasses perched on her slightly oversized nose. 'This is a fancy thing, what do I do?' she asked, taking in a dangling plastic stick attached to the machine by a curly wire.

'Scribble anywhere using the stylus and it will come trew.'

'I love your accent, where do you come from?'

'Exeter,' he said.

'Oh, I thought you might have come from somewhere else?' Philippa was from an older generation often tarnished with naïve racially insensitive comments, and though she recognised a need to be impartial, even that effort could fail.

'Yes, I was born in Lewisham, London.'

'Oo it's so difficult to do your best handwriting,' she said, changing the subject, embarrassed.

'It doesn't matter, anything will do just as long as you've signed.' The signature was representative of a scrawl; she was not happy with her effort.

'Let me do it again, I'm not happy, this looks nothing like my writing.'

The Rastafarian postman pulled the machine away before she could say anything more and returned to his red car emblazoned with the name of the postal service. He started to whistle again. She was left holding the parcel and instinctively turned it around, feeling the weight. She prodded the content for texture, squeezed it and then tried to bend it.

'What are you doing? It's not yours, put it down and wait for 34 to come back,' her husband said brusquely.

Frank had aged a little less well than his wife, despite being three years younger. They had married 43 years ago and sadly had no children. Chips, the tiny terrier had died recently and Phillipa now had to acclimatise to a different sort of animal, which took on the form of Frank and a cat. Frank was now at home all the time, having finished full-time employment. Like so many men of his generation, he had never planned retirement and had little to do. If one was to ask Philippa she might say, 'Well he could find a hobby and get out from under my feet.'

Philippa's husband loved his wife in his way but was frustrated with her nosiness and lack of skills in the world of technology. The little event with the delivery man was one such event, familiar to most of his experiences.

Phillipa and Frank did not know the woman who had moved into their small Dorset hamlet at number 34. There were five houses and the nearest shop was a mile away. On a fine day Philippa would walk the straight road into the village or use her bicycle, a heavy Raleigh with fixed gearing and a large basket on the front. When Frank was home she relied on him and his small car.

Phillipa went to make tea and heard the front door close. She entered the front room and looked out through the thin gossamer netting separating the window from the main curtains. She could hide behind this, obscured and yet see all that took place. A car arrived back at number 34 and Frank was making his way over to the opposite side of the main road. She saw a woman in high heels wearing a neat skirt and jacket. Philippa watched as the woman shook Frank's hand and took the parcel from him. Annoyance replaced surprise as she watched aghast as Frank was handing the stranger the very parcel that she had intended to deliver.

As Frank returned through the front door, Philippa rebuked him.

'You know I was going to deliver the parcel to the young woman myself; I wanted to meet her and maybe invite her over for tea at the weekend.'

The neighbour had only lived at her address across the road for six weeks. There had never been an occasion until now for an excuse to make more comment than seeing her car disappear or arrive back each day. Sometimes she stayed away. If this seemed odd, neither Frank nor Phillipa had commented.

Frank sat down, looking pleased with himself. He picked up his newspaper, sipped the tea Phillipa had made and ate one of the three custard cream biscuits he always had with his tea. After his first bite he mumbled, 'Not to worry, dear, it was no trouble. Have you seen this? Another car was stolen by kids too young to drive. Cars are dangerous things in the hands of these *tearaways*.'

Phillipa returned to the kitchen to suppress her frustration in private and left him to the paper. She set about making the evening meal, usually set rigidly for 6 pm. If it was not on the table promptly, Frank went into one of his moods.

The next day, a different caller came to the house with another parcel. Phillipa signed the machine, looked at the parcel, a little more confident this time, and noted the name. 'Ah, we had one of these yesterday from the same company.' She noticed the curved arrow which she thought looked like a smile.

'Yes luv, Amazon has grown into a popular online shopping provider,' he replied helpfully.

'So what is this "online" thing, don't you ring up or write a letter or something for the order after looking at catalogues?' He chuckled. 'This is the 21st century, my dear, no one does that these days.'

She walked back in and put the parcel down. Frank looked up from his newspaper.

'Another parcel I see? Who's it for?'

'Number 34,' Philippa replied. 'Did you find out her name yesterday?'

'No I didn't. She seemed in a hurry and I didn't want to hold the lady up,' he replied.

She tutted and nodded her head. 'Typical,' she said to no one in particular as she entered the kitchen. Men, they just overlook the details, she thought to herself. By the time she returned to the sitting room, Frank had gone. So had the parcel.

'Looks as though I am not going to get a look in,' she informed their black and white cat, who looked up as the clock struck 3.30 pm. A horse came out of the hole in the box and neighed on the half-hour. She hated the damn clock. It was cheap and typical of Frank to fill their house with cheap, useless items.

Frank came back shortly.

' What's her name and what does she do for a living and why does she have so many parcels from the Amazon place?'

'How do I know? I just let her have the parcel. She was in a hurry.'

Philippa again felt frustrated. She seldom lost her temper and usually deferred to her somewhat domineering husband. To accept his actions in this case and without fuss did not sit right with her. She wanted to know more.

Some six weeks later, she was attending her Women's Institute meeting. There was a lecture on the virtues of the internet. The lady speaker talked for forty minutes. Many of Philippa's WI members seemed indifferent, but

Philippa was mesmerised. She asked a few questions and found out that there were courses where she could learn about modern technology. Maybe she could learn something that Frank knew nothing about. That made her chuckle. Over tea she found five of the women used the so-called *internet*, but most seemed frightened by the technicalities of computers and the complexities of the names used such as gigabytes and running speeds. The RAM, or memory and operating systems were beyond many.

'Oh no, Philippa,' said a lady a few years older. 'I think we have to leave this complicated system to younger people. I have heard it is so easy to make a mistake. Someone ordered a garden kneeling cushion and found out she had ordered a garden bench when it was delivered. She then had to work out how to return it. Oh no, the internet is not for me, I can tell you! Ha, ha, ha.' She giggled at her joke.

While parcels kept arriving, not every package was delivered to Frank and Phillipa's address. Sometimes Betty or Terry Gould who lived next door had a parcel delivered to their house. At other times, the lady across the road herself was there.

Philippa persuaded Frank to take her into town shortly after the last WI meeting. She was going to attend a short five-week course but decided to withhold some of this clandestine activity from her husband. She knew he would kick off and ridicule her. Inside, emotionally, she felt she had grown a little bug called 'independence'! Part of this feeling of self-assurance came from the fact that an elderly aunt had left her a small sum of money. She almost felt guilty, like she was breaking the law, when she had opened her own bank account. Frank had always insisted they had a joint account. Philippa could now see the possibilities of the internet. She could even do her banking online. There were so many opportunities she could engage with.

The motor journey was only eight miles. Frank met an offset T-junction in his car. 'Oh Frank, you have taken the wrong turn,' she scolded gently. 'Did you not see the sign, dear?'

'Yes, of course I did, but this way is a shortcut.'

Philippa was dubious. Although he had seen the sign and had thought it was the right way, it wasn't, and Philippa corrected him at the next junction. Frank escaped any further interrogation as a tree branch had partially obscured the sign. Of course he pointed this out to his wife and she accepted this unconditionally.

'So how many more parcels have you delivered to number 34?' Frank was nearing the destination where Phillipa was attending her meeting on computers.

'Oh, you mean Deidre Hathaway. Yes, I have delivered a couple more to her. She is charming you know and works in Dorchester.'

'Oh, so you do ask questions after all?'

'Well of course I do!'

'What does she do for a living, and is there a Mr Hathaway?'

Having reached their destination the conversation ended abruptly as Phillipa climbed out of the car.

'I will see you back in two hours then, all right dear? And don't bother Mrs Hathaway will you?'

Frank grunted and drove off in his tiny car, crunching the gears.

Over the weeks, Philippa was inspired and came away from her course with more confidence. Frank had used computers in his work, perhaps unusually for the early 21st century, they did not have one at home. Frank picked up his newspaper one afternoon, magnifying glass in one hand, while Philippa sat down with something in her hand and quietly worked away. Curious, Frank dropped the pages and looked over, waving the optical instrument.

'What are you doing there?' he asked.

'I am just working online and searching the internet,' she said confidently.

'You're doing what?'

'Searching the internet,' she said.

'What, with that thing?'

'Yes, it's a computer.'

'Don't be daft. Someone has sold you a dud!'

'No they haven't, this is a tablet.'

'A tablet, sounds like something from the pharmacy.' He chuckled to himself at his stupid joke. 'What is that and what do you know about computers? Computers sit on desks and have keyboards and you have to attach them to telephone lines.'

'Yes dear, if you say so, but Wi-Fi connects this.'

'What planet are you on now? And where did you get this information?'

'I've been attending a course on computers and in particular learning about this type called a tablet. They are discreet aren't they, and connect to a box.' She pointed to the box with its flashing lights.

'When did that come?'

'I had the telecom service set it up when you went to bowls yesterday.' She had been desperate to get Frank out of the house. It had taken a while, but he had finally taken to something resembling a hobby.

The next day, a parcel arrived for Phillipa. It was some gardening gloves—her first purchase from Amazon. The postman delivered the package this time. He knew Philippa well enough now, having delivered the post for some time.

'Morning Mrs B. How are you today?' said the
Rastafarian. 'I see you're joining the Amazon family
around here.'

'Yes John, about time I joined the 21st century I think.'

'Well, everyone does it these days. No doubt I will see
more of you then if you keep this up.'

'Very likely, John.'

Frank noticed the Amazon label on several deliveries to
their house and seemed disappointed as most appeared
for Mrs Phillipa Bryant, his wife. Even his birthday
present came by way of the internet. Phillipa informed
him it saved on their petrol bill, which was not getting
any cheaper. The next day a largish parcel came
addressed to Dr Dennis Hathaway. Philippa laid hands
on this immediately. Frank had not seen the van arrive,
as he was in the garden attending to his potatoes. They
were supposed to have been peas, but he had misread the
packet. She noticed a letter from the hospital addressed
to Frank. She opened it up, as the stickiness on the fold
had loosened so that it could be peeled open with little
effort. Having read the contents, she placed it back in its
envelope. A good deal seemed to be answered by the
content. She made sure it looked untampered with and
 put the letter on top of Frank's daily newspaper where
he could see it easily.

'Another package for the lady across the road I see,
Frank, only this is addressed to Dr Dennis Hathaway.
Perhaps Deidre's husband is hiding over there. Ought
you not go and find out?'

Frank failed to read the letter from the hospital. He
moved as if a blur, disappearing swiftly out of the front
door, crossing the road with the speed of a
septuagenarian athlete.

Philippa noticed the time. Frank had been over the road for longer than usual, so she decided to take the bull by the horns. Crossing the straight road that had almost certainly been built by the ancient Romans centuries ago when they had invaded Britain, Philippa followed her husband's path. Ensuring nothing was coming along, she proceeded toward the two people standing alongside a sleek sports car.

'Hello Deidre, we have not been introduced. I think my husband has been keeping you all to himself.'

Phillipa felt the grip of Deidre's hand was firm but it was her Adam's apple that bobbed up and down and voice that gave the game away. Frank looked at his wife.

'No my dear, Deidre thinks it was an accident, she's not married but they spelt her name Dennis, what idiots.'

Phillipa studied Frank. It was clear that he could not hide his fascination for the tall, shapely woman who he seemed to idolise. Over the last few months he had had more contact and conversation than had been conveyed when she had cross-questioned him.

'Come on, Frank, leave Deidre to get on.'

'Nice meeting you.' Deidre smiled again, as did Phillipa. Their eyes made the type of contact that conveyed rather more information in such a short period than could be conveyed by simple words. Frank left reluctantly.

Yet another day went by and the doorbell rang. Frank was up out of his chair in a split second. He opened the door and was staring at a bunch of flowers. 'Oh, I thought you were the postman.'

'No dear, I'm the florist. Delivery for Bryant.'

'Er, thanks,' he said with disappointment.

'Who is it?' shouted Philippa from the kitchen. She was on her tablet looking something up. She enjoyed the fact that you could find recipes, look up words and facts, locations and even theatres and cinema times.

'Flowers,' Frank replied.

'Who for?' she shouted back.

'I don't know.'

'Read the label then.'

'For Bryant from, oh... Deidre...'

Frank had dumped the flowers on the table and left the door wide open. Philippa came into the lounge, saw the flowers and looked at the label. They were for her, not Frank. She noticed, or rather felt, the draught left by the open front door and then heard the sound of wheels squealing, a thump and then a car engine accelerating away. Silence followed.

Some of the neighbours gathered around the crumpled body of Frank. He lay there at an odd angle. Deidre was bent over, feeling his neck and checking him.

'What are you doing, Deidre?' Philippa asked, dazed and disorientated.

'It's okay, I'm a medical doctor, Philippa, but I'm afraid Frank is dead. That car failed to stop. There is nothing anyone can do about Frank, but we ought to wait for the police. Could someone get a blanket please?'

Philippa finally came back into the house after being given a cup of tea by the Goulds who lived next door. Deidre seemed to take charge.

Philippa's tablet lay on the table where she had left the machine. It had not powered down. The screen still shone...

'TRANS WOMAN'
FROM WIKIPEDIA, THE FREE
ENCYCLOPEDIA

A TRANS WOMAN (SOMETIMES TRANS-WOMAN OR TRANSWOMAN) IS A TRANSGENDER PERSON WHO WAS ASSIGNED

MALE AT BIRTH BUT WHOSE GENDER IDENTITY IS THAT OF A WOMAN. THE LABEL OF TRANSGENDER WOMAN IS NOT ALWAYS INTERCHANGEABLE WITH THAT OF TRANSSEXUAL WOMEN, ALTHOUGH THE TWO LABELS ARE OFTEN USED. TRANSGENDER IS AN UMBRELLA TERM THAT INCLUDES DIFFERENT TYPES OF GENDER VARIANT PEOPLE (INCLUDING TRANSSEXUAL PEOPLE).

...She sat slumped in Frank's armchair. She heard a crunching sound and realised she was sitting on an envelope. Frank had failed to open the letter from the health service. The outside had 'Dorchester Hospital' written on it in red. She opened the letter again, despite knowing the content.

Dear Mr Francis Bryant,

Thank you for seeing Mr Callaghan last Wednesday 23rd September. We write to inform you of the diagnosis of peripheral vision loss caused by scotoma related to the deterioration of the retina affecting both eyes. We recommend that you make a further appointment with our clinic to discuss the implications and any treatment. In the meantime, you are advised not to drive and must surrender your license immediately as you are not safe to drive. You are required to tell the Driver & Vehicle Licensing Authority (DVLA).

Eye Department, Dorchester Hospital

'I really must have Deidre over for that cup of tea,' she muttered to herself.

Author's Note

Dealing with numerous issues in 'Obsession' was fun, and the original story entitled '*Amazon Women*' first penned in 2017, makes up my story behind the 'marriage contract'.

The arrival of parcels ordered online is an event that excites us all. Maybe it is the latent thought of Christmas come early. The loss of sight has many deep-seated implications, and until this happens, those with average visual ability cannot begin to imagine the disruption to one's life. I saw this after my father lost his driving licence. The loss driving can be profoundly distressing and fundamental to our sense of independence.

Reckless teenage drivers were once a familiar sight, but less so today in a modern society where dysfunctional children and families still exist.

I chose to introduce transgender as this is a challenge for people to adjust to sensitively.

Philippa's brush with John the Rastafarian is yet another example of behaviour problems brought about by colonialism and anachronistic attitudes to colour. All of these issues impacted our fictitious couple, who, although married for 43 years, represent the all too common problem that arises after one retires. Frank and Philippa are certainly not alone.

David R Tollafield

THE SALESMAN

Ray immediately noticed the shudder of pain that shot through his knee joint as he opened his car door. It felt like dried up ball bearings grating inside. He grimaced and straightened it up with a crunching sound. The knee clicked and the pain subsided. Ageing was not a friend. Maybe now he should regret his sporting days, but he was a stubborn cuss. He closed the door, having flipped the back open, and as he reached into the trunk a voice interrupted his thoughts. He hadn't seen the man approaching.

The man was short in stature and had a slightly curved torso, giving the appearance of a barrel chest. His slicked-back grey hair appeared oiled so each strand separated into a mini corrugated arrangement. His face was red. The man started to speak breathlessly.

'Hello.' He leaned against the side of the car. 'Gordon's the name. We're neighbours; Gordon Little,' he said puffing a little less now that he had rested.

Ray, usually alert, would have spotted him but Gordon had taken a route which had cut across his pristine lawn, making little sound. The freshly-cut grass had that lovely summery smell. Ray loved this time of year, and could do his abstract thinking while sitting on his lawnmower.

'Hello Gordon, I'm Ray Mitchell.' Although his manner was not quite as enthusiastic as he made out seeing that Gordon's footprints had smudged the neat parallel lines he had lovingly made.

'Fine, fine thanks, thought you might like to come over for coffee, not that instant rubbish in the tin. Martha has just bought one of those new machines.' As he spoke, his tongue clicked, devoid of saliva brought on by a constant dry mouth.

Unsure what to say, and caught off guard, Ray realised the man was just trying to be friendly as he had moved into the house across the road that week.

Ray and his wife, June, were Gordon and Martha's nearest neighbours. Unusually, this was the first time Ray had seen either husband or wife. He agreed with as much good humour as he could muster and felt sure June would agree. In some ways it pleased him to think he had made the first contact, as he was usually the last to do so. June often accused him of being a little reserved.

'Well, that'll be fine; when?' Ray added officiously.

'Say tomorrow – and bring your missus of course.'

And that's how it started, a friendly greeting and neighbourly spirit. Ray Mitchell and his wife, June, met with Gordon and Martha Little and all seemed to go well for a while. Gordon insisted that they met up regularly so coffee became a BBQ and then a meal around a table with tablecloth and wine. June leaned over to Ray and whispered, 'They really are still trying to make an impression.'

Sipping his beer, he swallowed and responded in a quiet voice, 'But who are they trying to impress?'

Later, whilst in the kitchen, June and Martha stopped talking and listened in. They could hear the boys' voices getting louder.

'Tank corps, that's me, corporal. Suppose you were a major or something like that, you look that type?'

'No, I wasn't part of the armed forces—'

Gordon interrupted, 'So you've never fought for your country then?' Gordon was alluding to the so called Falkland's War or any of the conflicts the UK had become embroiled in.

'Hardly. My work took me elsewhere.'

'Oh yeah, what was that then?'

Ray's face took on a look of disdain. Gordon's cigarette turned bright orange as he pursed his lips tightly to draw in the drug. He inhaled deeply, allowing a dribble of exhaled exhaust to exit, blowing so he could use the period for effect.

'As a matter of fact, Gordon, it's none of your damn business.'

That was the first spike in their relationship. June and Martha looked at each other, having stopped their conversation about children and the fact that the local news had reported school meals were going over to a voucher system.

Martha returned to the sitting room with June where she could see the conversation was warming up. She attempted to make light of the topic - 'Come on, Gordon, not everyone is as passionate about wars as you, or obsessed with those long passed!' Any attempt at humour seemed lost.

'So, are you some sort of Conchie or what?' pressing the point home and ignoring his wife.

'I'm not sure all men who fought in conflicts have to fight. I'm pretty sure we can assume a good deal of non-combatting has been done behind the lines, and Ray may have been employed in something else. Bear in mind dear it's not like the last big war.' she tried to add helpfully, not being put off.

Martha's gentle intrusion, but firm tone caught Gordon off guard. He would have reacted more aggressively if Martha had contradicted him. Not willing to give up, he continued.

'Come on mate, you've got military written all over you. Perhaps you were you in the secret service? You know, subterfuge and all that stuff like at Bletchley Park? P'raps you had to sign the Official Secret Act, the one brought in during the Second World War by Churchill.'

By now, Ray was irritated at Gordon's manner, but even more so by his ignorance, let alone the continuous usage of the slang 'mate'.

'The Official Secrets Act wasn't introduced during the Second World War, but before the First World War.' He emphasised the 'S' on 'secrets'.

'Oh, so then you were a secret agent, like one of those that they dropped into France; what did they call them, SEO wasn't it, Special Executive Order? Part of the secret service MI5. Now they used them in the First World War, but they were only used in France. Come to think of it, that woman, you know the one that got killed by Jerry, she was an SEO person wasn't she?' Reinforcing the statement, rather than as a question, he continued trying to impress Ray with his knowledge. 'You know they made it into a film in fifty-eight, *Greta Garbo* or something?'

June looked at Ray; she had seen that expression before. A man she loved for being placid 99 times out of a 100, but then there were these moments. She understood and hoped diplomacy might win out. It didn't.

'Look, you silly little man. It was SOE, Special Operations Executive, not SEO. And it was not a branch of the secret service, neither was it just used in France but all over, including South-East Asia. Secondly, the film you mention was about Violete Zarbo not Greta Garbo. Garbo is an actress.'

'Keep your 'air on, mate,' betraying his London accent. 'Yeah, well I knew it was something like that,' he added, trying to account for his error yet sound correct. The cigarette flared as his lips dragged the last minuscule tobacco elements from the stub held between his stained yellow fingers. 'You know your stuff, old mate, reckon you were in the military though.'

Gordon was unconvinced and reckoned his nose was sensitive to Government personnel.

'And, DON'T CALL ME MATE! MY WIFE IS MY MATE!' Ray barked back, finally losing his composure.

'Well you're getting right shirty today, aren't you.'

As Martha and Gordon were getting ready for bed that night she said, 'Gordon dear, you do let Ray get under your skin.'

'Poncy bloke, thinks 'e's better than me just cos 'e drives a Jag. Worked my way up and made something of it. Head of section last year, I run the South-East now.'

Gordon sold a variety of knitwear. He was a travelling salesman and now headed a team. He made good commission and was successful enough.

'Well I'm sure he's done well too. You mustn't keep taking jibes at him. Nothing good comes from infighting, and they're our neighbours, remember.'

'Why doesn't he tell me what he does though? I'm sure he works for some secret service department.'

'I'm sure he will all in good time, but maybe he just doesn't want to tell you.'

'Maybe, but I reckon the snotty nosed git is hiding something.'

Two weeks later, Martha was pushing her trolley in the local supermarket when she bumped into June. 'Hi, how are you? Haven't seen you about since we last got together.'

'Hello Martha, day off work?' June replied, smiling.

'Only the morning, I'm on "lates", presently. That's the problem with this business, the shift work in hospitals, takes its toll. Thought I would get the shopping in.' Both women decided to go to the local tea shop and have a sit down and chat.

'Look, June, what are we going to do about the men? They're forever arguing.'

'It's difficult, both are proud and they like to think they're right.' June did not believe this, but knew if she broke diplomacy with her female counterpart, all sorts of problems would arise. Inside, she told herself what she thought of Gordon, but she went for preservation of peace for now. Do they give *Domestic Nobel Peace Prizes,* she wondered?

'I couldn't agree more with you, he's got this hang-up over Ray's occupation. It just niggles at him that Ray won't share it. Gordon has told Ray that he's a regional sales manager for clothing. We just wondered why Ray wouldn't open up a bit.'

'Well, I'm not sure anyone has asked Ray about his occupation so directly before. The conversation seemed to come down to what he did or didn't do for his country. I mean, you have to understand Gordon seemed to be accusing Ray of dereliction in his duty.

But, if you want to know, he works in security. You know, dealing with alarms and locks; nothing that fancy really.'

Martha laid out Gordon's 'tea' that evening. She thought nothing of the meaning behind the term 'tea', which the British would style as a meal. Gordon would have a snack at lunch, but his breakfast made up for his lack of a midday meal. Martha usually cooked him bacon, sausage and eggs before going to work.

Excited at the thought of her successful detective work, her face lit up with a smug smile.

'Guess what? I now know what Ray does.'

'Yeah, go on...?' his mouth full of food.

'He's in security, fits alarms and does locks. I think he's upmarket and does it for expensive properties.' Gordon was still chewing while considering this information, savouring his steak and mushroom pie. His teeth slowed their grinding as he leaned over to pour more tomato ketchup over the meal. He stirred the sauce in, turning it into a morass of reddish goo.

'So what's all the secret stuff about then? Maybe we could get a deal on this house? Anyway what sort of security does 'e 'ave? I've seen no cameras or alarms. 'E should have the confidence in his own product.'

If Martha was aware of his clipped words, she took no notice, despite her better elocution. Gordon kept pondering as he chewed. Martha watched him, wondering what was percolating through his mind.

'First on the estate. In fact he told me on one of his bragging trips that he owned the estate...' He chewed, grinding the meat so the result of his mastication looked like the contents of a cement mixer when his mouth opened up like a carp.

'Or, was it the land and he built the first house while it was still a field? Set up on the rise there. It's like he's lord of the castle. Long drive and wide front garden, tall wall and lights. No dog though. One child called Samantha all growed up.'

'And what's your point, Gordon? You're talking in riddles.'

Gordon's mind was doing overtime.

*****

Ray felt good to be out in the fresh air as it was bright and quiet on the fairway as he prepared to line up for the second hole at his local golf club. Several hundred yards away Ray could hear a rustling noise. He played the shot. Colin, his golfing partner, complimented him.

'Should be good, you might make it in two further holes.'

'Wanna bet, old fruit? Here's a tenna that says I'll do it in one.'

'Done.'

The noise became louder. It was the sound of material rubbing, and it turned out to be a man wearing a bright yellow plastic anorak.

'A friend of yours?' Colin asked.

Ray turned slightly and saw a hand wave thirty feet away. His hand came up more by reflex. Gordon, appearing as a bright coloured beacon, was heading straight for Ray.

'Damn, it's that silly little man who lives opposite me. Gordon Little. It's a joke, he's five foot seven and his name's Little. He's little in stature and little in brain.'

Hello Ray, how nice to see you,' Gordon said.

As Ray repeated back, Colin looked sceptically at Ray, 'Er...and you Gordon,' muttering under his breath. Gordon's face was suffused a purple red colour and he was puffing, breathing with difficulty.

'Hey… just a moment, got to get my breath back,' he said sucking in more air.

'What brings you here?' Ray asked without humour.

'Joined the club and thought I would try my hand at golf.'

'Have you played before?'

'No, but never too old to learn, eh old mate?'

Ray swallowed the sobriquet, mate, inwardly seething at the coarse term.

'This is Colin, Dr Colin Webster, he's one of the local GPs at the health centre.'

The two men shook hands, Colin looking at Gordon. He noticed the white hair, the chalky grey skin and the slightly cyanotic lips.

'Haven't seen you at the surgery, Gordon, who's your doctor?'

'I go to the other surgery across town, Doc Smithers, you probably know him?'

'Of course. Do you smoke?'

'Yes. What's this, a consultation or something?'

'Sorry, an old habit of mine. Can't help it. You just looked a bit unfit to be racing around the golf course, and the smoking could explain it.'

'Well, that's my business, isn't it. My dad lived to ninety and smoked forty a day, never came to any harm.'

Colin looked at Ray, and then back at Gordon.

'Sorry,' Colin added politely.

'Mind if I join you?' Gordon said without intending to take no for an answer.

If Gordon had any sense of embarrassment about crashing Ray and Colin's game, he indeed showed absolutely no regard. Both had played at the club for ten years and had decent handicaps.

'So have you got a handicap allocated yet?' Ray asked.

'Do I need one?' he smiled.

'Er yes, if you want to play at the club, so they can pair you.'

Colin interrupted the flow and suggested they all take a shot at the second hole and allow Ray to follow on.

'We've put a tenna on me getting this in after my second shot. Care for a wager?'

'Why don't you stand down on this for a moment?' Colin suggested reasonably.

'Nah, tenna's good, but what about me getting it in three? Let's say twenty?'

Ray thought this was like taking milk from a baby. I can't lose, he thought.

'Yes, okay, that's good for me.'

After the agreement had been struck, Ray pushed in his yellow tee and placed the ball on the hollow. He pulled out a No.3-club and positioned himself. The shot went wide. Colin didn't do so well, but curiously, Gordon, who had never played before, had a good eye. The club hit the pitted white Slazenger ball, looping smoothly in an arc and covered the whole distance to land on the smooth green.

'Bloody hell,' Ray exclaimed. 'I thought you said you've never played before.'

Gordon smiled. 'Not on this course!'

Ray parked his car in front of his garage and swung his knee out cautiously. It was sore again, but not as sore as his mood and pride. He stormed into the house and the carefree, smiley greeting his wife offered was lost. She saw he was troubled.

'Darling, what's the matter? How was golf?'

'Don't ask, but if you want to know that little man was there. Implied he didn't know how to play. It only turns out he has a handicap of six. Took fifty quid off each of us, the smug bugger.'

'I haven't a clue what you're talking about, handicaps and such. Shouldn't you have been a better sport?'

'I'm off for a shower,' ignoring her last comment. Half an hour later Ray's mood seemed to have smoothed out, gin and tonic in hand.

'Our tickets for the Caribbean have arrived. Maybe that'll cheer you?'

He opened the stylish blue travel wallet and saw a pair of airline tickets—first class. Two weeks in the Caicos Islands would suit him.

Gordon entered the kitchen and Martha looked up

'So, they're off on holiday. Do you know where?' he asked.

'Yes, the Turks and Caicos for two weeks.'

'So they're going to Turkey then, wonder what the weather's like? Never did trust those Turks. Fought against us in the First World War, you know.'

Martha ignored him and put a cake in the oven.

'Colonel, this is impressive. No smell and leaves no trace,' a tall, imposing man with a moustache and an impeccable clipped English accent boomed.

'Yes, General, the whole structure is silent and once in place it seals the room.' Brigadier General Sardis seemed pleased with what he saw and heard.

'The outer wall is put up first and cranes slide the metal panels in. The mechanism is built into the roof so it's invisible and panelling manufactured around this. Two Henson motors drive the four walls. They're silent. A back-up power unit runs off the mains electricity as well in case of power cuts. We are trying to work on a solar model presently. Sensors are infra-red and set off the mechanism. The inner skin, which includes the doors, hides the panel. Look at this model.'

Ray pushed a small pointer through a scaled model door, setting off the mechanism. A metal screen came down, covering the windows and door of the model. He pulled off the roof and could see the small motor used to power the apparatus.

'What about the full-size concept? Has it been tested?' The man from the Ministry of Defence held a document in his hands and started to turn the pages. Sardis has personally overseen this particular defence contract.

'Can it be done for this cost, Colonel Mitchell?'

'As long as the price of aluminium doesn't change, the remaining components are straightforward enough.'

'We've been tasked with protecting the most sensitive locations in the network, and this structure should allow us the added benefit of not just security but entrapping any would-be intruders.'

Joss McKinley, Ray's engineer coughed. 'Er, sir, can I say a few words?'

The large workshop took up thousands of cubic feet. Despite being divided into different sections, an echo still reverberated from one end as a hammer hit metal and a machine rumbled into life. Noisy though it might be inside, the building was scrupulously clean. Army standard, of course.

Colonel Ray Mitchell was an engineer working on security for MI5. He was a civilian, but retained his title, as allowed in the British army. The contracts were of course secret, and naturally, people like his nosey neighbour were not privileged to know more than the type of information June had passed on. June herself only knew the cover story.

'Ah yes, Lieutenant McKinley, fine work. What is it you want to say? Hopefully not that you have had second thoughts?'

'No, no sir, but I do want to point out that this is a modern, highly technical rat trap. Once those metal screens are down they will seal the whole internal space like a can of jam. No oxygen. Once the existing oxygen has depleted, any intruder not released within twenty minutes will suffocate.'

'Yes, Lieutenant, I was aware of this but we are talking about extreme espionage. This is going to work for us. If the Russians can use Novichok, we can use something a little more refined, don't you think?' the Minister replied.

'Well, it's a question of what you think is refined. A fast poison is kinder than suffocation maybe?' McKinley said.

'I'm not paid to worry about collateral damage, Lieutenant, just getting the job done within budget. The Cold War still exists in our view, but of course this is a project contained within the Official Secrets Act, as you know,' Sardis said.

'Any more concerns about the effectiveness? I want a demonstration of a full-scale model so I can take this back to the PM who has to sign it off,' Sardis added.

After Ray had seen Brigadier General Jeremy Sardis and The Minister out, McKinley turned to his boss. 'Christ, he's a cold fish. Usually they worry a bit more about collateral damage, I thought, Ray.

'Well he seems pleased, anyway,' he continued. 'Let's get a demonstration set up. Seven days from now okay?'

'I'm out of the UK if your recall?'

'Ah yes of course, well-earned I'm sure. Leave it to me, Ray, I can carry out trials in the meantime. Is that okay?'

'That won't be a problem. Anyway that's why we have a site prepped. We can use cameras to monitor it.'

'So will that be site sector Whisky-Bravo-Echo or Whisky-Bravo-Charlie?' Joss asked.

'Whisky-Bravo-Echo is our preferred location as it has dummy material which has been leaked through the usual routes so foreign listening stations can pick up coded messages.'

'Good, well I am sure all is in order and I can leave this in your capable hands, Joss. I'll look forward to catching up when I get back.'

'Give my best to June and have a great time,' Joss added scribbling down 'WBE'.

'Will do, bye,' Ray walked out of the hanger-like building toward a modern block where his office was situated. He headed up this division for the armed forces no longer in uniform or part of the regular army, but it was all off the books. Ray did not like to wear a uniform, primarily because of the sensitive work that included a wide range of materials, be it tanks or sensitive documents. These days it was computerised units. With the Cold War at an end, and the Berlin wall dismantled in '89, the latest man, Vladimir Putin, was now in the Kremlin for the long haul. Britain's response toward security had to be maintained, and there had been enough embarrassing leaks. Ray had already predicted that cyber-attacks could affect computer systems, even though this seemed a long way off. He went to his meeting, then continued working late as tomorrow he and his family would start their holiday.

The family were driven by Jeep into the village of Bambarra on Middle Caicos Island. A golden-white colour adorned the smooth stretch of sand with beautiful clear tepid seas; thankfully it was outside the hurricane season. The cliffs of limestone contrasted the coastline. Ray gave little thought to Gordon and Martha 4000 miles across the Atlantic in the UK as they swam and sank through the clear warm waters to explore the seabed and multi-coloured coral.

It was the dead of night. Gordon slipped out of the back of the house, the luminous dial on his watch indicating twenty past two in the morning. The blackened face reduced any reflection, but the boot polish kept irritating his throat.

Martha was fast asleep, snoring in fact, so he was assured she was in a deep slumber, having taken a sleeping pill. He realised that he had been overzealous with the application of his polish, which smelt rather high with the resinous paraffin-based paste. The taste on his tongue caused him to spit. His dark clothing hid him from the moon overhead and although not full, it still acted as an overhead lighting system. He eased the gate open and saw a faint light on the house that stood above the estate. He assumed the Mitchells had left this on to deter burglars. If Ray had a secret occupation, so had Gordon.

A small fence obstructed the view from the road and he climbed over, catching his leg on a loose nail that must have been sticking out. He swore softly, trying not to give himself away. Upon climbing the steep, neatly coiffured grass bank, he slipped on the damp surface. By morning, a frost would no doubt make this worse. While the temperature was cool, his energy and fast pulse rate kept him warm; a bead of sweat ran down his nose. Brushing the droplet away, he felt a cough. Nearby bushes had a sweet smell and tickled his throat. He swallowed, and the threat that would have caused him to make a noise passed. The moon illuminated his path as he made it to the back of the house. As there were no houses here, but fields and a nearby wooded area, he was now in the clear.

He had previously surveyed the property when they had visited Ray and June. No alarm boxes were evident, although a security light suddenly shot out a beam of bright white light, so he pulled himself into the shadows. He doubted anyone would bother with this. Two-thirty-five illuminated on his wrist informing him of the time. Ten minutes so far, he told himself. The light went off as he was out of reach of the sensor. The back door was wooden and had a simple mortice lock. This confused Gordon.

'I thought Ray was a security expert?' he thought. He pulled a small case from his back pocket and selected a strange-looking object. After inserting the skeleton key he found it failed to work, so he then picked a second, then a third key. These were crude fashioned pieces of metal that allowed him to push and twist where space allowed to fool the tumblers in some locks that it was the real key.

His effort paid off as he heard the click and the lock released. Once inside he could use his torch and fed his way through the utility room where June did her washing. The door was closed but not locked. Making his way through the kitchen, he located Ray's study. Again the door was shut but not secured. The eerie silence didn't worry him. A clock ticked loudly in the nearby lounge. June's mother's grandfather clock was massive in size and solid wood with a teak veneer. He would have liked to have searched around other rooms, but he focused deliberately on the study.

The oak desk was some eight feet in width and four feet deep. Light pierced the louvred window, sending horizontal lines across the surface. He approached the desk from the seated position and pulled at each drawer. All opened easily. Again this seemed strange. Maybe there wasn't anything important after all? 'Right then, maybe there's a safe?' he thought.

He focused on the walls. There were no paintings, but a couple of framed drawings and pictures. For the most part, the objects on display appeared representative of Ray's past travels. He went to the picture frame, and felt around it's sturdy edge, easing it forward. The picture pivoted smoothly on a hinge, revealing a heavy metal door with a keyhole. From one of his pockets he selected a small box. It was magnetised and so clipped easily again the metal safe door. He pressed a button to turn the selector on and illuminated digits whizzed around. Once the mechanism had stopped he twisted the handle of the safe and the heavy door swung open. He detached the box and with a smile glanced at it celebrating the efficiency of the technology for such a small object that he had been loaned. The red coloured emblem had been scraped flat so no one could make out the markings or identity of the manufacturer.

'For someone safety conscious, Ray's security is appalling,' he chuckled inwardly. He found an envelope and retrieved it, surprised that nothing else was kept in the safe.

Could there be another safe? Was this a decoy?

The envelope was stiff and yet thin. Turning it over it measured 4.5 x 6.5 inches, the type used for personal communication. As the clock chimed, he jumped involuntarily letting out a curse under his breath. His breathing quickened and he tried to steady his pulse. Thoughts of a cigarette entered his conscious mind. He turned around to see if there was anything further that could quench his growing curiosity. A click sounded a distance away, then a faint whirring noise. Confusion wrinkled in his face. A shadow appeared over the window, and the illuminated light decreased. The room was dark as a final click occurred. It was as if a curtain had come down in the auditorium of a theatre. Silence descended while Gordon started to gain some sense of alarm.

Gordon looked down at the brown envelope and tore it open. His eyes grew larger in the dark as his torch made out the words on the back of a photograph. The picture showed three men in uniform. The colonel, centred, was unmistakably Ray Mitchell. By now his thoughts were confused as he tried to work his brain; for some reason he was gasping for air. Taking long steps, he raced to the door of the study and found it was hard, smooth, cold and resistant to his efforts to enter the gap where the open door had led him from the hallway. He thumped the solid panel hard becoming more anxious by the second. His heart raced again and his eyes bulged. A pain shot into his chest.

Martha woke up to find the other side of the bed cold and empty. By mid-morning, she became anxious and called the hospital to tell them she would not be in, giving few explanations other than family matters. By mid-afternoon she called the police. And so began a long list of questions, with the police basically telling her he was a grown man and that he would no doubt return soon. Two days later her call was taken with a greater degree of concern and a police presence finally appeared.

The car arranged by Brigadier General Jeremy Sardis for the Mitchell family arrived at the country hotel not far from Ray's work, an old RAF location requisitioned from the Second World War accommodating high-ranking visitors for clandestine activities.

'Ray,' June asked, 'where are we going and why are we not going home directly?'

Ray opened a note sent by Joss and it simply told him, 'PROBLEM. WHISKY BRAVO CHARLIE ACTIVE.'

'Surely it was Whisky-Bravo-Echo that was activated? Whisky-Bravo-Charlie was due to go operational later on.' Puzzlement sounded in his voice.

June heard him whisper but could not make out the words.

'June, don't worry, there's been a burglary at home, nothing stolen, no damage but the police are crawling over it and Sardis suggests we stay at a hotel on the firm.'

'Oh no, are you sure? Mum's jewellery was in my drawer, I should have put it in the safe.'

'Really, nothing's missing, I promise.'

A non-descript black estate had arrived, at which point Gordon, shrouded in a black body bag, was pushed into the back on a collapsible trolley. Neighbours appeared as ants from the woodwork; the word passed like Chinese whispers.

'Gordon Little, no, surely not...'

'Such a nice man...'

'What'll poor Martha do now?'

Martha was a mess and needed comforting. She had been picked up by her sister and decided to pack a bag until the commotion ebbed. Her sister helped as much as anyone could. The midday radio news reported:

Sudden death.

A man was found dead two days ago, after his wife reported him missing. Gordon Little, a salesman for Gosling & Gosport was found in Mr and Mrs Ray Mitchell's house. Suspicious circumstances are not suspected. A post-mortem is expected later today.

Ray sat in a chair in Jeremy Sardis's office. He handed Ray a sheet of paper with a note from the Minister.

'As you can see the Minister is delighted. The live experiment was a complete success.'

Ray scanned the note, and indeed, as far as the Ministry of Defence was concerned, this was an ideal result.

'But when I left, Whisky-Bravo-Echo was the location selected, not Whisky-Bravo-Charlie. I mean to say, Jeremy, the location WBC was not even active.'

'Ah, yes, it was supposed to be inactive, but then MI5 alerted us.'

Ray looked down at a photo pushed across the desk and saw an image of his neighbour, Gordon Little. It was an older picture and his white hair was dark brown.

'Little was in the Tank Corps in catering, but he spent time in the glasshouse, having stolen army property and selling it on the black market. It seems his army days were spent somewhat differently than he made out. Once a thief, always a thief. By all accounts he wasn't a bad one.'

'Did his wife know?'

'It is doubtful that she would've known as he did hold down a job as a clothing salesman.'

'And the police?'

'Well we have a preliminary report which finds nothing strange about his death, except that he died of a heart attack; coronary thrombosis to be precise. The doctor's note says he had an infarction which killed him.'

'Did he get into the safe?'

'Yes, we found a sophisticated box which he used to find out the digital code to the safe. This was almost certainly Russian as the lab boys and girls identified the Commie 'Hammer and Sickle', despite all efforts to remove it. We also found your note on the back of a photograph. Of course we retrieved it before the police got hold of it, thanks to those wide-angled camera lenses you incorporated into the surveillance system.'

Jeremy continued. 'The point is that his doctor, Dr Smithers, confirmed that Gordon Little had heart disease because of his smoking, an account corroborated by Dr Webster, who I believe you know? We managed to suppress the pathologist's report, or should I say produce a second report altered slightly for our benefit.'

Ray thought back to the day Gordon had appeared at the golf club out of breath.

'So, what you are saying is that he broke into my house and died of natural causes? Why alter his report then?'

'That's the size of it, yes, but MI5 have uncovered another link, which is why WBC was activated. It seems that Gordon bumped into a man who worked for the Soviets which confirms the high tech equipment he used. His contact was British born but used as a go-between. The man has been arrested and the missing puzzle pieces completed, so we have shut down the espionage link.

'You ask about altering the report. Fair question. Once starved of oxygen the heart would have to work harder, and his lungs would try to absorb what little oxygen was available. He would start to build up carbon dioxide and this would register when his lungs were examined, as they were indeed. Asphyxiation would then be a question raised by the coroner. I had the report lifted and replaced with the help of MI5.'

Ray nodded an understanding, but then added, The break-in was no accident then, but an attempt to locate information about Trap-W-B?'

'We switched the live demonstration to your house – WBC. As you know, the Ministry owned the estate before you moved in and constructed the Trap-W-B as version alpha before any other work could be completed, or the build seen by prying eyes. The low-key security was deliberate of course, as the Trap idea was to isolate and neutralise someone first, leaving the event appearing as an accident. This incriminates the burglar as the guilty party. Mr Little was in the wrong place at the wrong time, or from our point of view, the right place at the right time. The Ministry is delighted. We have now broken a Soviet ring so our defence method has been validated and remains above legal suspicion. Used only for strategic targets where security is important, we have a vital weapon in the Cold War.'

'This is post '89 Jeremy, there is no Cold War as such now.'

'Oh, I wouldn't be so sure.'

Ray stood up and shook Jeremy's hand firmly.

'I hope June enjoyed the holiday. We'll have to get you over so you can show us pictures of the Caicos. Ruth will love that.'

'Sure, I look forward, bye then.' Following customary handshakes, Ray left the General at his desk to answer the phone. As he walked, he turned the card over that Sardis had returned to him. The photo alone had been left in the safe. A picture of him showed his two good friends who had all joined the SAS together, a fact that Gordon would have recognised moments before his life expired. Ray recognised them as casualties of another time; one killed in Iraq in 1991, the other Joss 'Mack-the-knife' McKinley. All three were wearing a sand colour beret with a badge that depicted a dagger with wings.

Ray smiled at the two words he had typed neatly onto a label stuck to the back of the photo that Gordon had seen. It simply said:

SORRY MATE!

Author's Note

My next-door neighbour was a kind man and played his part in the Second World War as a tank driver. Later he became a salesman and regional representative, and a successful one at that. He riled my father with many of his pedantic ways. He loved golf in retirement, smoked incessantly and died of a major heart attack. We felt his loss. I am grateful to him for allowing me to build the character from his wonderful memory, as I know his sense of humour would have extended to my taking such a liberty.

Having started with the second world war I realised that Ray and Joss would have been much younger and so I placed them in the SAS and the first Iraq war (1990-1991).

Ray Mitchell was loosely based on my father, although he had nothing to do with the military – it was his brother who did a little work for one of the secret services in the high tech business.

My father and his neighbour clashed many a time and father would say they did it to get a reaction from the wives!

THE WITHERED HAND

Anna typed up a contract. It was a simple case of conveyancing, but her boss Jane Masterson expected it done correctly. As a qualified audio typist, the 48-year-old didn't do much traditional dictation these days or use her other skills. It was all audio and dictated onto a digital dictation machine. Spiky pencil strokes of Pitman shorthand on reporter pads and mini cassettes had all but died out. Voice-activated dictation software was starting to replace some secretaries, but Jane, a traditional lawyer, valued an efficient secretary. Anna had trained on typewriters when she left school at 17. At first there were clanky, clunky ones. Then there were electronic versions, and then there was the personal computer or PC. Even in her lifetime, technology had created significant changes. She had once thought of becoming a medical secretary, but had decided to avoid those complex Latin names associated with medical conditions and terminology.

Typing skills and employment used to be about speed in terms of words per minute. If you managed over 45 words/minute then you could usually find a well-paid job. Anna could hit 80 words/minute which was exceptional. Well, she could once, but over the last month she had to keep stopping to rub her hand. Francine, her colleague, friend and fellow typist at the Redditch firm of Masterson and Jensen, made up the second full-time secretary. Fran's skills included office management as well, and she was therefore technically senior to Anna.

'I see you've stopped, Anna. Hand hurting again?' Fran asked.

'Yeah, the electric shocks seem to be worse today.'

'Anna, you ought to get that seen to as it's starting to affect your work. Repetitive stress syndrome and all that. You know it can affect typists.'

'I know, Fran, and I will. It's getting me down.'

Anna was married to Jim and they had a single child, a daughter now aged 22 called Bethany. Jim was a site foreman and worked for a builder while Beth was at university studying law. She sometimes worked at Masterson and Jensen's for experience and pocket money. At 48, Anna's thick, wavy hair still broke across her shoulders. However, she had started to add colour to the grey strands. She had mild short-sightedness and used glasses for work, as she found she was experiencing headaches related to the constant use of the PC. Other than this minor concern, she enjoyed good health and still cut a good figure. She googled the hand condition and found out that it was not as uncommon as she might have thought.

Jim and Anna had a fairly traditional marriage. She went to work and came home and did the housework, cooked and had taken care of their daughter's schooling before she'd left home. Jim had done some of the trailing around, dropping off and picking up with their daughter's busy social life. Of course that was all before Beth had left for university in Manchester. Why she had gone to Manchester Metropolitan University rather than Birmingham Anna didn't know. Had she been in Birmingham then she could have stayed at home and saved money. Travelling in by train was easy, as there were good connections with their small town of Alvechurch.

'Try Karl Rufus, Anna, he's an excellent specialist. My sister used him when she had a problem with her hand,' Jane Masterson, her boss, said, after Anna had told her about the shooting pains in her hand. Jane was good, provided you were honest with her in the first place.

'Thanks Jane, that's useful. I'll see what my GP has to say.' And so Anna made an appointment to see her doctor.

Dr Sidwell was her doctor at the local practice. It was rare these days to see your registered GP, or even see the same doctor twice in a row. Dr Sidwell was a senior partner in the surgery and she had known him for over 20 years. It was no insignificant matter that seeing a GP today could be hit and miss. Locums were temporarily employed and filled the yawning gap that had started to grow in British medicine. Without the vast import of doctors trained outside the UK, the medical profession would have diminished further. To put it bluntly, which doctor you could see at short notice was a lottery. Anna knew she was lucky to have Matthew Sidwell. He knew the family and had supported her through her pregnancy with Bethany. Today he examined her hand, pressing into the palm.

'Ah, yes, I think you have median nerve compression. How long have you had this, Anna?'

'Three months I think, but the tingling in my fingers is worse and I can't grip with my thumb like I used to.'

She explained how it affected her at work and said it was getting her down. And so it began.

Sitting at the dining room table at home, she dished up Jim's evening meal. He took sandwiches to work and then ate a cooked meal in the evening. Jim treated Anna well, but the disproportionate split in their domestic workload was common even to younger couples. Anna never dwelled on the problem, although a good few of her female friends voiced their opinion openly about equality for her gender.

Jim was well-built. At nearly six foot he stood seven inches above Anna. Her husband was a gentle and patient man. Liked by his bosses and workmen who he supported professionally, he was decent and understanding. Anna used to say of Jim to her friends, 'He's my *gentle giant*.' Their marriage was by most standards a good one.

'Anna, I've got some bad news.' Her appetite suddenly waned. She hadn't even discussed her GP appointment that day. He stared at her as he funnelled some of the battered fish into his mouth, making sure he had her attention. 'Ron says he's selling out, and while the workforce can be transferred to the new owners, there's no guarantee everyone will have a job. Of course many labourers are only taken on contract by contract, so like the gig market they will move on.

'I think we'll be okay though,' he said, noticing that Anna looked worried. 'The new firm will need foremen, at least those with experience, so I'm not worried. It just means a slight change.' He didn't tell her that he might have to travel further afield than the West Midlands.

Typical of many wives and mothers, Anna put her health problems from her mind and they talked about what was happening in Jim's life, the latest tweet from Donald Trump and the Uighur Moslem problem in China. Neither of them usually took much notice of foreign affairs, and China was far away. Jim merely said that Trump hated the Chinese and thought a war could break out as relations had been deteriorating in the China Sea with Taiwan. The US was stepping up their warship presence.

Anna had good days and bad but her hand was getting no better and it was starting to affect her whole arm. Dr Sidwell had injected the hand which hadn't help much, so he sent her off for a test. It comprised pictures taken similar to those when screening for pregnancy and the baby's position in the womb. The results showed changes associated with the nerve that Dr Sidwell had mentioned earlier.

'H'm,' he chanted, sounding a bit like a Buddhist in prayer, and while looking at his screen he said, 'The wonders of modern technology, Anna, images all straight from the hospital these days. Makes such a difference. Well then, the report seems to be positive. I'll send you to the hospital, as the exercises, injections I've given you, and now the ultrasound scan shows that we should consider whether surgery is needed.'

'Ooh. Surgery. Is that necessary?'

'It's only a simple procedure really, and carried out under local anaesthetic.'

'What? You mean like a dentist's injection?'

'Yep, stay awake job. Excellent. You'll be back home same day.'

'Erm, okay. That's sounds reassuring.' She paused and said, 'Could I see?' Peering down at a piece of paper she'd pulled out of the capacious soft brown leather bag that she treasured, 'ah yes, Dr Karl Rufus. My employer recommended him,' she said.

'Ah yes. Karl. Good man, and specialises in hands. He's a plastic surgeon. Good if you want your boobs doing!'

Sidwell used the humour typical of the older medic, which today suffered considerable disdain and was un-PC. Anna bridled a little at this supposed joke, mainly because she could not tie up her nerve problem with human breast enhancement. If Sidwell noticed anything, he certainly showed no response and just carried on. 'Anna, Mr Rufus,' he started and continued without explaining that Karl was no longer a doctor from the hallowed Royal College of Surgeons and had therefore dropped the title 'Doctor'. 'Mr Rufus only works in the private sector now. Obviously making enough money to turn away from the NHS, eh!' He followed this bit of banter with a chortle. Anna just about understood what he was saying, and again assumed what most would think. Like many, she knew little about the way medicine worked in the UK. In the USA, while complicated and a country with less open access to medical care as a nation, the idea of an insurance policy was more acceptable than in the UK where there was an attitude of *I shouldn't have to pay*. Anna was concerned about seeing someone less reputable.

'Hey, Anna, your mind seems to be drifting.' The balding doctor smiled, showing his dimples. He tapped her hand lightly. 'Any problems?'

'Er, well is he, I mean is the man you're going to send me to any good?' Anna assumed it would be a man, as she didn't know of any female surgeons.

'I'm sending you to Mr Anwar. He's an orthopaedic surgeon and very clever. I send him all my hips and knees.'

'Yes, but this is my hand, not my hip or knee,' she pointed out, her face belying the concern with a wrinkled brow.

'Look, he's qualified and does all kind of surgeries so you'll be fine. He also works privately and does hands there. Does that make you any feel better?' he smiled.

Jim took Anna to the hospital by train on Tuesday, 21st January 2020. The weather was dry enough and was comfortable but cool at around 44 degrees. The big Queen Elizabeth Hospital had 1215 beds and was relatively new at ten years old and named after the Queen's mother, also called Elizabeth. Parking was possible, but as Jim and Anna lived at Alvechurch it was easier to take the branch line into the city. The main reception directed them to Area 4 until they were called.

'Mrs Taylor?'

Anna looked up. 'Yes, that's me.'

Jim attended with Anna, and they were placed in a consulting room to await Mr Anwar.

'Hello,' a young man said. He wore a slightly creased striped shirt without a tie, dark trousers, and his brown hair was cropped short at the sides. 'I'm Mr Randall, Mr Anwar's registrar.'

Anna looked disappointed not to see the consultant.

Randall informed Anna he would be looking after her, and asked to examine her hands. He glanced at the records, noted the letter from Dr Sidwell and glanced down at the questionnaire Anna had filled in, in reception.

'Just eyesight problems, no operations, no allergies, taking no medicines,' Randall fired off.

Anna nodded but then said, 'I'm taking pain medication for the hand when it gets worse.'

'Any sleep problems? How much does it trouble you?'

'No, it only causes me problems when I pick things up. You know my grip is weaker than it was. I have dropped a few things and I cannot type as fast as I could.'

'So your occupation is affected then?'

'Most definitely,' Anna said.

'Right, wait a minute.' Mr Randall left and went into a secretaries' room. Of course Anna and Jim were unaware of what was said.

'Jess, I've got a carpal tunnel I need to schedule. How are we looking? Can we fit her in? I need a couple more *hands* for my logbook. For some reason this group of patients keep going on someone else's list.'

Jess the secretary checked her computer linked to the Day Surgery schedule.

Henry 'Hal' Randall was a senior registrar with moderate experience, having taken his Royal College Fellowship so he could make decisions and lead on many of the outpatient clinics, as well as running theatres. Naturally, as with all registrars, he needed sufficient experience to apply for the top consultant's post to complete the vital completion certificate in surgical training.

He returned to the room. 'You're lucky. We've had a cancellation for March and we can fit you in,' he lied.

'That's great, Doctor, er I mean Mr Randall. I thought I'd have to wait a long time.'

'It's not always true, Mrs Taylor, that the NHS keeps people on long waiting lists.'

'My nurse will give you some information to read about the surgery.'

'When can I go back to work?' Anna asked.

'Oh these operations don't take long to recover from.'

'So I can start typing in three weeks?'

'I need you to sign this form,' Randall said.

Anna and Jim looked at the yellow double-sided sheet with a tear-off carbon copy.

'Is this a type of contract then?' Jim asked. Randall seemed to be in a rush and wanted to get away. He grunted. 'No it's a consent form,' he replied curtly.

'But this tells us what we can expect like a contract. I mean, if my wife signs it, what guarantees are there it will work?'

Randall's eyes narrowed. His thoughts were dismissive and he became impatient.

'There are no guarantees, Mr Taylor, this is surgery. I've written down the risks. If your wife does not want to take any risk then don't sign.'

Jim looked at his wife.

'Risks? I thought this was routine surgery,' Anna said.

'It is, but even routine surgeries carry risks. Look, ask the nurse if you have any queries but I've got an emergency to deal with so I'll see you on the day of surgery, okay? Ask any questions you want?'

Randall was out of the door as if the room was on fire. The section on risks contained two lines of spiky, illegible writing in black ink. Anna turned to the nurse. 'What does this say? The writing is hard to decipher.'

Infection, healing delay, swelling, stiffness, numbness and pain.

'I suppose these are not common then?' Jim said.

'You'll have to ask the doctor I'm afraid.'

'But the doctor... Mr Randall said to ask you.'

'Well, I don't work in orthopaedic surgery. I am just filling in today as we are short staffed, so I'm not qualified unless it's your plumbing system...' Seeing the Taylors were confused, she clarified her little joke. 'I work in urology, you know, with people's waterworks.'

March came around quickly, as did something else. It was called the coronavirus, with the complex name SARS-CoV-2, shortened to Covid-19. Jim and Anna had been aware of an outbreak in Wuhan, as had everyone else. The Chinese Government notified the US on 3rd January, but it was not until now, 11th March, that the World Health Organisation announced a pandemic.

Back at the office Anna realised she was no longer pulling her weight.

'Do you think this is likely to affect us?' Anna asked. Jane and her law partner, Ted Jensen. A meeting had been called because of the new rules, which included all the secretaries and junior lawyers, to consider the effect of the news on the firm.

'We still await more information from the health secretary, but Anna, you are going in to have your surgery on the 19th so we expect you off work for around three weeks. Is that right?'

'That's what my doctor has said, yes.' Anna's mind drifted back to the appointment at the QE Hospital with Mr Randall.

Anna had googled the condition and knew Randall's three weeks might be a little on the short side compared with published views. Some said up to 12 weeks, but Anna felt Jane Masterson would prefer Randall's prediction.

The days crept closer to 19th March, and as they did the UK's death rate increased. The word 'monitoring' came up and decisions were required.

Jim drove Anna into Birmingham for her operation. She was in and out within the afternoon and back at home with her arm elevated in a sling. Minimal pain medication was required at first. Three days later she had to attend the doctor's surgery, as her hand had become infected. Antibiotic tablets settled things for the next week. Her stitches had to come out earlier to help drain the infection and so the gap in the wound widened. Premature removal of these sutures caused the incision line in the hand crease to enlarge. 'It is quite sore at times,' Anna told the practice nurse.

'When do you have to go back to the hospital?' the masked practice nurse asked. She longed for a visor and thought this whole thing about PPE, the protective gear staff wore, should have been more adequate as she was in the front line.

'It was supposed to have been the 16th April but you know with this virus it's a problem. Although Jim will take me in at the drop of a hat as he is at home presently.'

'Well look, Anna, call us if you need help and we can always fix up a telephone meeting with the doctor. It seems that this is going to be something all practices need to consider.'

Three more weeks of lockdown and deaths rose to over 10,000. Jim went out to clap the NHS, something that had taken the nation over to raise morale. Anna of course could only stand and watch; her hand was still painful. By mid-May, Jim was on furlough payments, along with 10 million others in the population. Anna was technically on sick leave as she had not returned to work and now received statutory sick pay of £95.85 a week. It was now eight weeks since her operation, and if anything she thought the hand was worse. By July, Anna was regularly popping pills for the pain. It was only by sheer perseverance she could tolerate sitting masked to have her hair done now that hairdressers were open again. The weather played on her pain. Her arm was mottled with blue discolouration and was incredibly sensitive to touch. While her original pain arose in her hand, the whole arm now was affected. The hand had swollen through disuse. Typing was now impossible.

Relief came in tears at the announcement of her follow-up appointment. It was 29th July. Four months since her surgery. She looked at the smooth shine to her hand's texture. Her wrist had flexed inwards and seemed stiff. Any movement or sudden loud noises caused her agony. The pressure on the family was incipient but still impacted on their relationship. Jane Masterson had been sympathetic and said that Anna should let her know as soon as the consultant had seen her. They did need to know how much longer she would be off work. Jim was back in the building business, but now in Manchester, while Beth had returned home to isolate, which seemed ironic as she was also studying in Manchester at the Metropolitan. Beth did what she could to support her mum, who she believed was going crazy.

Beth drove her mother in her father's car to the QE Hospital for her follow-up appointment.

'So, it was good to see Aunt Megs yesterday, Mum?'

'Yes, it was nice of her to come over from Stafford. She looked well.'

Megan was younger than her sister and had spoken to Beth outside the house. She inhaled the smoke from a cigarette.

'Want one?'

'No Megs, I've given them up but lord I could do with one for the stress in my life.'

'So, what do you think about your mum?'

'Christ, you've seen her. She's a mess. I want her to sue the hospital for negligence.'

'Seriously do you think that's going to help her with all the crap this virus has brought, what with Jim away and Anna in so much pain?'

'I don't know, but it can't be right. Having been left so long and the problem is getting worse. Even Anna's doctors don't know what's happened. Her kitchen drawer is full of painkillers which are sending her doolally!'

'Have you said anything to her about this?'

'No, not yet but I thought of contacting her boss to see what she thinks.'

Beth decided to see how things played out and insisted that she attend the clinic, knowing that her mother would struggle independently. They were taken through quite quickly, which surprised them. The waiting room hardly had anyone in it and all attendees wore masks.

'What seems to be the problem?' a junior doctor asked Anna, grabbing at her arm.

She pulled away in agony, tears in her eyes. 'It bloody hurts, I can't sleep and my arm feels stiff at all its joints. It's cold and clammy and my life's shit.'

'Sorry!' the doctor replied. 'I'll get the consultant.'

'Christ, he looked as though he was just out of school,' Beth said. 'I hope he didn't do your surgery.'

A short man entered the room with an extensive waistline. His shirt sleeves were rolled up. His mousy hair was brushed back and thinning. He wore rimless glasses, appeared cleanly shaven behind his mask and had a ruddy complexion.

'Hello, I'm Mr Mourib Anwar, the consultant. I understand from Danny, my SHO, that you are concerned after your operation.'

A SHO was a senior house officer and still had to take his Fellowship examination, while Danny was ranked as a doctor rather than a surgeon. Danny shrank back from the scene as he felt the two women were hostile. He feared saying the wrong thing which could later be used against him or the hospital. Medico-legal cases consumed the coffers of the NHS regularly. Additionally, one of the nurses told him incorrectly that Beth was a qualified lawyer. Danny did what most would do and sought his senior's help. Mr Randall would have been his immediate senior, but Randall had made himself scarce.

Anna's tears had stained her face. She had lost weight and every movement exhausted her. 'Please don't hurt me.'

Mr Anwar had the sense to ask her to show him any movement that she had and expose her arm rather than use any forced movement as his junior had done. The limb was discoloured and had wasted. The skin looked different to the opposite hand and arm, and the texture was significantly different. The muscles were thinner on the operation side, and Anna was holding the arm stiffly to avoid movement.

'Any problems with your left arm or hand?'

'No, that seems fine, it's just the right hand I write with.'

Anna's hand was swollen and stiff. She could not use her fingers, let alone grip anything. Anwar recognised the problem and knew this was not going to be an easy conversation.

'Er, I'm afraid you have a chronic pain problem that comes with the name complex regional pain syndrome. We shorten this to CRPS. It is not common, but it can occur after injury and surgery. Mrs Taylor, the truth is that we don't know why some people have this problem and others don't.'

'But it will get better won't it?'

Anwar had heard this so many times. He knew that usually it didn't get better at this stage of deterioration, and could worsen. Covid-19 had affected routine appointments and Anwar knew this had delayed optimal management. In the UK, the support network for CRPS was poor compared to many other medical problems. He explained all of this to Anna in layman's terms. Mourib Anwar was from the old medical school, having trained in the late seventies, but he also had compassion. He was about to continue when Beth spoke. Her voice was business-like.

'My mother has been waiting months to see someone. Given the lack of progress leading to her impending disability, we believe her treatment is negligent.'

The room was so quiet that one could hear a conversation next door.

Mourib Anwar gathered his thoughts and said, 'I can well imagine this is in your mind, and frankly it is easy to see how you have come to this conclusion. Are you medically trained?' he asked Beth.

'No, I am a student studying law.'

'Many have tried to sue hospitals for this condition and all I can say is it takes a long time, even with the best lawyers. CRPS is not a condition that is easy to prove. Generally medics don't give such advice but persistent claims that take three or four years to come to court only make matters worse. More so if the complainant loses.'

'You sound as though you've been there.'

'Yes, Miss Taylor, I have. It never ends well for patients, in my experience. The best we can hope for is to see my colleague Dr Christine Mandrake who runs a clinic in chronic pain management.'

July and the months that followed were warm, and the nation seemed to get back to a sense of normality as Covid death rates declined. The NHS was slow to re-emerge and after a two-month delay, Anna saw Christine Mandrake. Dr Mandrake was an anaesthetist but ran the pain clinic. She confirmed the diagnosis that her orthopaedic colleague had offered and tried to put into perspective the need to have both physiotherapy and psychology support, as well as pain support. 'I want to up the dose of medication you are taking. And I want to use stick-on patches that will deliver more pain relief. Because of Covid, we cannot get a support group together, but we are working on a Zoom-based meeting.'

Dr Mandrake was warm to Anna's problems and ideas of her suing anyone were soon dispelled by the pain doctor. Beth was not so sure and decided to speak to Jane Masterson. By now Anna had lost her job and knew she could no longer work as a typist.

'Dr Mandrake, could they amputate my arm to take away this burning pain that never goes away? It's like, well, like putting your arm in a bucket of boiling water and being unable to remove it from the heat.'

'You poor woman,' Christine Mandrake said. 'I know it sounds like a solution but believe me it isn't. In the latter part of the 19th century, undiagnosed pain was first observed amongst wounded soldiers during the American Civil War. It seemed as if damaged nerves caused an excitable reaction. Amputations were routinely performed and in turn the casualty suffered further pain. No, amputations are not a good idea, so put this out of your mind.'

A follow-up appointment was issued and Anna genuinely felt a little elated. She liked Christine, who understood a good deal about the condition, and her treatment started to work. Then a letter came through the post. Anna used her left hand to open and read the letter.

Dear Mrs Taylor,

We are sorry to cancel your next appointment. Dr Christine Mandrake sadly passed away having caught Covid and we are trying to find a replacement to support our patients. This inconvenience is distressing to our pain patients and we understand this is the last thing you need. We will be in touch as soon as we can arrange a further appointment for you.

As she read the typed note, tears streamed down her face. Was it the loss of her specialist that meant so much to her, or was she selfish? Maybe she was sad that such an excellent doctor had died in her prime. She was Anna's age. Then she was at a low psychological ebb in her life and could see no future without years of pain ahead. The Prime Minister, Boris Johnson, announced a second lockdown. Anna had found the first hard enough, and with the thought of the second she felt empty inside.

Jim was sleeping in a different room and Beth wanted her to take legal action. The strain on all of them was telling. Masterson had said there was a chance, but she needed a hungry firm who took no prisoners to work on Anna's behalf. Masterson said some patients were destroyed when they failed to achieve a successful legal settlement. Anna knew money would make little difference. Feeling that her life now in ruins, she then made her final decision. It was the only route she knew she could take to achieve resolution.

Stafford railway station was not far from where Anna's sister Megs lived. The station served one of the busiest routes through the county of Staffordshire. The station lay on the junction of the Trent Valley Line and supplied London in the south and Manchester in the north, as well as Birmingham in the west. Five platforms out of seven were dedicated to passenger transport and high-speed trains. Anna left Megs at 11pm. They had drunk two bottles of wine and Anna had pre-arranged a taxi to take her home. They hugged and kissed. Megs said,

'That was fun, we must do this again.'

'Of course, little sister.' But Megs did not see the tears that had fallen onto her older sister's cheeks.

Loaded with painkillers and a fresh fentanyl patch, Anna descended from the taxi.

'You sure, lady, this is where you want to stop?' the driver said.

'Yes, I'm being picked up here,' she lied.

'Well, you be careful. It's late and there's funny people about you know.'

The gap in the fence was not easy to find, but there was a full moon and she could make it out. She stumbled a few times and slowly reached the bottom of the bank. Recent rain had not made it easy and mud smeared over her yellow coat and dark trousers.

She stared at the deserted metal lines that ran from north to south and back. There was an eerie silence. The smooth gleam of the moon reflected the silvery metalwork that highlighted the frequent use by the trains designed to reach 125 miles an hour on this stretch. The alcohol and infusion of drugs caused her to sway, but she eventually found one line. This line was the London track. She lay down and pushed her head and neck over the thick, cold, unforgiving structure and waited.

There was no reason for Maajid Ashiq to have stopped. It was 2 am and traffic was light. Having competed his last fare that night, Maajid was passing the point where he had left Anna at the point she had asked to be dropped. For some inexplicable reason he slowed his car down and pulled on the handbrake, leaving the engine running. He leaned over the metal fence and saw a train coming at speed, at first with two small peeping lights in the distance. The lights on the train appeared to grow larger as he looked at the approaching train. The speck in the distance had started to brighten.

The yellow figure lying on the line was only too familiar to his tired eyes. A train covering the distance of one mile at 125 mph would take two minutes. He knew he had to do something, but his hip was painful and awaiting an operation. He found it awkward squeezing through the gap, owing to his rather generous waistline. He looked at the slope and realised this was another obstacle he had to overcome. Glancing up, he could see that the lights had now covered half the distance from when he had initially spotted the train. He braced himself, trying to build his confidence. Athletics was not one of his pastimes. Those round yellow eyes looked brighter still, and he knew time was running out. He hit the slope and tripped, rolling a short way. The ground was wet and soggy, softening his impact. He found himself at the bottom and looked up to see the front of the train now but yards away. He stood up and yelped in pain as his ankle twisted. The train screamed past. The dimly-lit carriages made a streak of light, the inner space not easy to make out. The wind whistled as the speed pushed the air around the track, causing loose leaves and waste paper to rise and spin. And then it was gone and silence remained. He reached for his mobile and realised it was sitting in the cradle on the dashboard of his car. He looked over and saw no movement. The train had disappeared by the time he had processed the information, the rear train unit becoming ever smaller. The driver would never have seen the woman, she was too low down against the ground. Often suicides would stand and the driver would be able to apply the brakes, not that this did much good as trains took a long time to stop. Drivers would often just feel a bump. The yellow features would not have registered, as many objects were yellow around stations.

The ambulance took a fraction over four minutes to arrive at the County Stafford Hospital A&E department as traffic at this time of the morning was non-existent. A police vehicle led the way—two sets of flashing blue lights with their accompanying sirens.

As Anna entered the casualty department with two intravenous drips, there were no less than five personnel around her. The ECG made the usual heartbeat bleep-bleep-bleep, indicating this woman had somehow survived. Miraculously her upper body was intact. However, she had no legs below the knee. The steel wheels had neatly guillotined her legs and cauterised the stumps. She was unconscious.

The orthopaedic registrar turned up. He was on call for trauma and the clock read 2.22 am. He rubbed his hand through his brown hair and then over his eyes, then stared down at the inert body. The face looked familiar. He moved closer and a shiver went up his spine.

EPILOGUE

The world was still counting the death toll and analysing data. Henry 'Hal' Randall had recognised the unconscious body from the QE Hospital in Birmingham earlier that year. He recalled the operation on her hand. More to the point, the dressing down from his consultant Mr Anwar, FRCS, was all too recent in his memory. It was not because he had performed the surgery poorly. Hal was competent at what he did. It was because he had not faced up to the post-operative requirements that all surgeons had to face. Such requirements dictate those in charge assume responsibility. He had deliberately disappeared that day Anna and Beth had come back with the chronic pain problem. Sending in Danny the SHO had been unforgivable, as the letter from the GP had made it clear there were problems. Hal had been ashamed, and so knew the history. He had transferred to County Stafford to be near his fiancé, but when Anna came in he was shocked. It took little time to realise that she had tried to take her own life.

The London southbound train was late and so the track she laid her head over remained free. Anna had not accounted for the earlier Manchester northbound train across whose track both legs lay.

Hal was not a bad doctor, but when the sister found him she saw an exhausted man, knees bent and his back cranked against the wall with his backside off the ground. Propped up to support his body the sound of his crying was heart-wrenching as he lost complete composure. She knelt and their eyes met as he looked up at the nurse. His eyes were red and watery with tears that ran unchecked through the follicles of his dark stubble. 'I don't think I can do this anymore...' he said.

Anna Taylor survived her suicide attempt, thanks to the emergency medical care given by Hal and the team. Six months later she took an overdose. As predicted by the late Christine Mandrake, amputation was not the answer. For Anna there would be no peace from pain. Suicide was the only way out. Hal left medicine and gave up any chance of becoming a consultant.

Author's Note

Years ago I was told a story by one of my anaesthetic colleagues from the same hospital mentioned. A man had tried to kill himself on the London line but had both legs amputated by the southbound Edinburgh train due to mistiming the trains. He survived, but more than that I have no idea. As this was many years before Covid-19 hit the world, my story rests on two facts.

Surgery and injury cause the most devastating pain in a rare number of cases and some consider both amputation and suicide. Complex regional pain offers no rhyme or reason as to who it attacks. With early multidisciplinary team management, early intervention can help positively.

The effect of Covid on the medical and health professions cannot evaluate the damage while most of the world remains unvaccinated. It will take years to mop up the debris brought by a virus invisible to the human eye. I make no apologies for avoiding any sugar-coating of a story embedded with misery.

To my knowledge, Stafford has not had this type of rail incident and the story is otherwise fictitious. Stories from train drivers are harrowing, and collateral damage extends to workers who have to clear up the remains of human bodies – that is if there is anything to clear up. I borrowed the title from a local author although this was called The Withered Arm. His name was Thomas Hardy (1840-1928) and once upon a time he lived 30 miles from my home.

For audiences with less knowledge of the British medical system - the GP, shorthand for general practitioner of medicine, is self-employed and holds a contract with the National Health Service or NHS. Enshrined within an Act of the British Parliament, the NHS started in 1948 and provided care for the whole nation. The GP is paid for each registered person on his books. In contrast hospital doctors are salaried without depending upon patient numbers on their case books. All GPs are doctors and qualified in medicine, while surgeons curiously qualified as doctors in medicine and then switched from the title Doctor to Mister. Modern surgeons have developed from barber surgeons and anatomists. Previously surgeons had a lower standing than the physician. Hence 'mister' has held since time began. Most people, including Anna, would call all medics 'Doctor'.

THE PISCARRO CONTRACT

NEW YORK, USA

It was patrol officer Eddie Durran's third suicide that
week. Last week it was a jumper from a bridge. At least
that was clean and the body was fished out of the
Hudson River before it became bloated. He'd seen
bloated before, and at times the skin split, leaving a
messy pulp.

The gas line explosion was a bit more gruesome,
leaving a family wiped out and looking like overcooked
BBQ steaks, all curled up and shrivelled. Today,
perhaps, was worse.

Joe Buczaki jumped in front of the commuter train
that morning, a journey that Joe would have taken from
his home to his office in the city. The train stayed on the
track, but when an 85,000lb metro car hits a soft body
weighing 200lb, the metro car wins. Buczaki was now
part tangled body parts. The head was no longer

attached, but ended up 100 feet away from the track, the eyes remaining open, staring back at the world. He was also now beyond accusation for a financial crisis that had all the hallmarks of America's stockmarket crash of 1929-30 when property had been over priced. An excess of large bank loans arose, as did debts. The housing market had been manipulated, a fact that was now evident. The year had now clicked from 2007 into 2008.

When the detectives checked Buczaki's house, they found no note. He was married with an eight-year-old son. His company had collapsed. He signed off high-yielding mortgage investments. A month later, his company filed for bankruptcy. The financial crash slowly took its toll at both ends, the middleman and the end user, the little guy on the street. Losses were mounting, not just in New York, USA, but in many cities worldwide. However, some wallowed in their new wealth, where others suffered painfully from greed or naivety.

Martin Piscarro felt elated. He had every reason to experience a high. Atlas Financial Corporation had made a great deal of money. He wondered how he could spend it all, but there it was. Good decisions made money, bad decisions cost you money. The excitement burst over him as he hugged his partner Anzillo in his office. Now back in his room the irritant on the phone was trying to burst his bubble.

'How could you do this to me?' Peter Elfin shouted down the phone at Piscarro. Peter was a middleman and felt the squeeze.

'Pete, you know the deal, you've been in the business – how many years?'

Elfin was not appeased. AFC had sold their shares early, made a killing and then the market had slumped.

'But we had a deal. What about the heads-up? You left me in the damn cold! What am I gonna tell my investors?'

'Well, in a world where time allows tranquil thought maybe, but selling and buying on the market seldom allows such tranquillity...'

'Think that's clever? You're a goddammed crook! I've lost millions overnight.'

'Peter, this is just business, it's nothing personal.'

'Fuck you, you'll soon get yours.'

Martin disconnected. Reaching across his desk, he pressed the intercom.

'Miss Williams.' It was never Sylvia, always Miss Williams; she was too senior to be called Sylvia. 'If Elfin tries to contact me again, ensure he doesn't get through.'

'Of course, Mr Piscarro, that'll be no problem.' Martin knew Williams had a tongue that could scoop the fungus out of blue cheese.

'Oh, and please get my wife on the phone.' Martin reminded himself to give Miss Williams a bonus, she would like that. She was worth it.

Piscarro never liked spending money unless it was on something like an investment, or someone he valued. That someone would always be a person who protected his back. His wife came into a different category; she and his daughter were deeply precious. Anyone else came second or third. At Christmas, it was his wife who gave the gratuities out to those who provided services. No-one gave him a tip. On reflection, he smiled at this thought.

'No, I give myself that.'

Kim Piscarro was irritated at waiting on the end of her line. The phone clicked and then her husband's voice echoed.

'Kim, good news, we can book that holiday you've always wanted…'

Something like elation sounded at the other end, a squeal resounding in a high-pitched sound. He pulled the handpiece away from his tortured ear. He outlined the success and hard work he had put in, leaving out that some felt indifferent to these methods.

'…yes, that's right,' he continued, composure returning to the person on the other end of the phone, 'pick anywhere you want, just make it expensive.'

Anzillo called Martin before he left for home. 'Say Mart, I think we caused a bit of a stir, damn Lehman Brothers shakin' the banking world. I think the shit's going to hit The Wall; hope it stays steady. Reckon we can outride it though. You have a good weekend now.' Anzillo rang off, his southern accent contrasting to Martin's eastern brogue.

Charlotte opened her eyes as light crept through her blinds. Sleep was patchy as she wrestled with the effects of her arthritis. She tried to swallow. Pain radiated through her jaw, something that had worsened recently. Turning allowed some control if she could use her side to prop up her weak body. Clawing at the linen sheets with her fixed, deformed fingers, she eased the bedclothes back. The sea of pain came in spasms as the inflamed joints reminded her of the agony the day would bring. Her mother had insisted that Charlotte move back home, and they employ live-in help. Charlotte sold her apartment reluctantly. Unmarried and now ineligible to work, her day was one of just coping, getting through tasks which most able-bodied people took for granted. The door opened and the help arrived.

'Charlotte, you should have pushed the buzzer, you know. I'm here to help.'

Rachel Gunter, an experienced nurse and physical therapist, was provided by an agency. Charlotte's father could afford the $2700.00 a week.

'I've got to help myself, Rachel. I know you mean well.' Her mouth, partially closed with arthritic stiffness, muffled her voice so it sounded as though saliva sloshed around as she talked.

'I've told you, I must support you. Your stiff back means using other joints that can't take the weight. I can massage the muscles and give you an injection.'

It was hopeless contradicting Rachel, who was way too experienced and mature to head off her pleas.

Getting dressed took time. Charlotte used an adult nappy to avoid making the bathroom at night. Rachel's room was next door, but the nappy gave a little freedom. Rachel bathed her charge. She ignored the personal matters that many would find unpleasant. It was a job and she put all unsavoury thoughts from her mind.

'That's it, slide over... I'll put the arm up after. You know the drill,' acknowledging the role of the wheelchair.

Rachel was always careful not to pull on Charlotte's arms and risk tension on her shoulders. Hoists in the bathroom helped. Her role was both cook and carer, cleaning up mess, dealing with pain, protecting the skin, helping her move and attending appointments with her. Unmarried, the 42-year-old had her work cut out. Nonetheless, she enjoyed her role and the house in the Hamptons was rather plush.

Charlotte eased her body into the chair as best she could. The custom stair lift made a quiet electrical whir, taking her from upstairs to the ground floor where she would eat breakfast and take numerous pills to make her life easier. She held on to the arm of the chair with her gnarled hands. Fingers stuck out like loose sticks from a bird's nest. Her feet, encased in soft shoes, hid the deformities and nodules that made walking cumbersome and painful.

'Like walking on pebbles,' she often said.

'There you go, a bowl of mashed up, warm-milk-soaked cereal, just what you like. Hold the spoon like that.'

Rachel administered, as if to a child. Charlotte was no child. She should have been in her prime. The adapted spoon helped those unable to grip, which Charlotte could not. Rachel took in her distorted fingers on account of the rampant inflammatory condition she had developed eight years ago. 'Rheumatoid' was the worst kind of arthritis that affected only a small percentage of people. Drugs were limited and many she tried had side effects. Her medical care cover, typical in the American middle class, had run out, so she depended on her parents. Martin, her father could afford it. Both parents were currently abroad, enjoying a holiday that her mother, Kim, had planned for some time. Naturally Kim's sole focus was on Charlotte, her only child. The break was no doubt welcome.

'Look, a card from Quito. Your mom has written as usual. Here, you read it.'

Rachel handed her the postcard showing the central square and guards where the President resided in the capital of Ecuador, one of the more stable countries in South America.

'Ah, they're off to the Amazon apparently,' Charlotte said. Her jaw had eased with the medication and massage, but her communication still sounded garbled.

Rachel nodded, opening any remaining post so that Charlotte only had to read the contents, or direct Rachel to throw it in the trash.

'How long are they away?' Rachel asked.

'The plan was three weeks. They're supposed to fly to Lima and then catch a flight to Cusco.'

'Wow, lucky them. Wish I could afford to go to such interesting places.'

'Maybe you will someday,' Charlotte suggested.

Rachel did not articulate her thoughts at this, but she could have said, 'Yeah, if I was not looking after a cripple 24/7!'

ECUADOR, SOUTH AMERICA

'Good God, look at the colour of that river! It looks as if someone has thrown chocolate into it; reminds me of that *Willy Wonka* film, you know the one with Gene Wilder and those orange dwarves,' Martin said.

'You mean the *Oompa Loompa* men,' Kim added.

'The colour is derived from the silt churned from the riverbed, and water running from the Andes,' a squeaky, high-pitched voice answered, but it was directed now to a large group of people trying to speak over the throbbing of the powerful outboard motors. Martin and Kim were not the only people travelling up the River Napo.

The tall, willowy Ecuadorian guide, David from Quito, had a strong Spanish accent. David had a lean face with a sharply-defined nose, and sported a dark growth where he hadn't shaved. His gelled, jet black hair shone, and was pulled back into a ponytail.

Two fibreglass canoes fitted with powerful twin Yamaha 50 engines pushed against the wild river, zig-zagging over the half-mile-wide waterway, avoiding heavy logs and other debris. Martin stared at the wake as the boat travelled at speed. The humming vibration from the engines made talking challenging. He turned toward the guide.

'So how far is the lodge?'

The customary name badges allowed David to name the speaker as Martin.

'Two and half hours, Martin,' David responded loudly over the engine thrum. The powerful outboards curdled the muddy brown river and divided the water effortlessly giving off a strong gasoline smell.

The canoe kept up a steady 30 knots making it difficult for Kim to keep anything focused when snapping pictures. As promised, two and a half hours later, the canoe left the main Napo River and they changed canoes to head up Anugo Creek by paddle alone.

'Thank God I can hear now,' Martin said as the engines were exchanged for paddles.

'Jungle is a word reserved for the edge of the forest,' David explained as they pulled away, making little noise. There was only a gentle trickle as the water ran by the hull with its forward momentum.

'We say galleria instead of jungle to emphasise the distinctive disorganisation of the flora. Thick plants such as water hyacinths influence the design of the river edge, which changes with time.' David the guide kept up a steady stream of information as the tourists spun heads this way and that, trying to capture all before them. The constant click of cameras, the occasional 'wow' punctuated the guide's running commentary. The creek finally opened into a lake that stretched peacefully across the basin with a wooden lodge set on the far side, appearing as a Disneyland fantasy. Having left their longer power boats behind at the landing station, their dug-out canoe bumped gently against a wooden jetty. A sudden screech from a bird broke the stillness. The water in front of the lodges standing on stilts was a murky colour, tinged brown and green from the fallen trees and foliage leaking their tannins. The surface otherwise remained glassy. The contrast to the main Napo was distinct.

'Hello, I'm Fausto, the manager of Anangu Eco Centre. This is Marcello, our barman. Help yourself,' pointing to a tray of cocktails. Each passenger carefully eased themselves out of their unstable boats, grabbing a wooden post that ran at intervals along the jetty. Fausto, David and Marcello made sure no one toppled into the lake.

'Now that's what I call service with a smile,' Martin said, sipping some coconut-based drink with a lump of pineapple floating on the surface. David had a leviathan knowledge of the Amazon basin, and after supper they sat on wooden benches and listened to him give a short lecture. Martin was unimpressed and wanted to slink away, but Kim was having none of this.

'Amazon was re-discovered by the Spanish and so named after the Aztecs sent them on a wild goose chase to their early deaths after fantasising about cities made of gold. This was a lie to trap the Spaniards, who succumbed to malaria around the 1540s...' While his English was good, he still had a strong Latino click on certain words. The PowerPoint presentation whirred away, its beam picking up insects that headed for the light source.

Kim and Martin retired to the welcoming protection of the mosquito nets that night.

The next day started early at 5.20 am, and as the canoes set off, the sky became murkier with darkening clouds bringing rain. The heavy blue plastic ponchos Marcello had offered were soon required. Unfortunately, the hoods allowed the mosquitoes to attack Martin and Kim's faces despite being covered in repellent.

'Mosquitoes like to come out when it rains. They replace the smaller insects,' David said.

Martin had pointed out that the small flies before had just been plain annoying, now the damn mosquitoes were vicious. He regretted suggesting Kim could go anywhere she wanted as long as it was Planet Earth. He would have preferred to have spent time in Hawaii.

'Stop grumbling, Martin, and look at this kapok tree.' The base was some four metres wide and had an expansive root system. The group continued picking their way over the muddy ground as the rain hissed, bouncing off the leaves as if from the head of a shower in reverse. Many large leaves reduced the deluge, but light was difficult and Kim struggled again with her camera. The group strangely looked like the Klu Klux Klan with their hoods obscuring their faces. All they needed were two holes for the eyes to complete the masquerade.

'These strangler trees, or Ficus as we call them, are the star parasite of the forest. Seeds dropped from bird faeces germinate in the canopy and send long, thin roots to the ground which then take hold. As the roots draw on nourishment, they grow, and become thick, twisting around the host tree until the host is killed. The forest is full of this activity, as well as lianas.'

'David, can I ask a question?' Kim said, interrupting his marathon flow of illuminating jungle descriptions. Those in the party closed up to listen.

'The Kichwa are resourceful I've read and make medicines from the plants...'

'Yes, Kim, you're right. Medicinal plants abound in the forest, offering many beneficial remedies. He broke the stem of a plant. For example, this would enhance wound healing,' he said as the sap oozed from the end.

'What about arthritis?' Kim asked.

The company of visitors emerged dripping from the forest. The surface of the lake was pitted with tiny explosions as rain disturbed the surface. By the time they arrived back at the lodge, everyone was wet through. Refreshed from sleep and a shower, Martin sat at the bar stool for a second night, taking in the mix of different people making up the lodge's guests. A gin and tonic rested in his hand, he scratched at a mosquito bite and thought of the next project with Anzillo. Over in the corner, a family of tourists were noisily discussing the day's visit to the galleria. Cindy had accompanied her mother, Betsy from Ohio, who laughed loudly. Her lips retracted showing a set of white palisades for teeth. Martin turned to look over at a couple called Bob and Lesley. Both were Brits with their funny accent. They said they came from Newcastle, wherever that was, although he had heard of New Castle County, but that was in Delaware. 'So what brings you here?' Lesley asked Martin.

'My wife. She's on the lookout for a cure for our daughter, but so far not much luck.'

A tall, well-spoken man sitting alongside his attractive blonde wife, interrupted the conversation. 'I heard your wife ask about medicines. You know we're hoping to see a medicine man, a Shaman, they call him, tomorrow.'

The man offered his hand, leaning in.

'Hello, I'm Einar Knutsen and this is my wife Berit.'

Everyone started to introduce themselves, just as Kim joined the growing party.

'Hello dear, let me introduce you to these people,' Martin said, now on his third gin and tonic and feeling pleased with himself for engaging with the company. Twenty minutes later, they settled down, fuelled by the relaxing mood. Imbibing wine, beers and spirits, they chatted about the day and in particular about medicinal plants and creepy bugs. The meals were substantial. Martin pushed something around on his plate.

'What's that?' he asked.

'That's cassava,' Berit said. 'It's toxic but not when cooked. Taste it, it tastes nutty, a bit like potato you know? The South Americans use it as it is rich in fibre and good for the diet.'

'How do you know all this stuff?'

Berit gave Martin a knowing look. 'I talk to the cooks and staff. They're very helpful.'

'So what do you do?' Bob asked Martin. Martin's concentration was still on the Viking beauty, Berit.

'Er, what?' he said.

Bob's wife, Lesley, was talking to Betsy. The conversation was rising in decibels, and fuelled by alcohol, familiarity was growing. Betsy's expensive teeth flashed at some joke. They were all sat around the same heavy wooden table. Howler monkeys made loud whooping barks in the far distance. An occasional thumping noise erupted from the lake, as a Black Cayman thrashed for a moment, no doubt spotting a piranha or small frog. From out on the lake, the humans must have sounded equally loud.

'I work in the financial sector, Bob, how about you?'

'I run a curtain shop, or did until the financial crash last year.'

'Oh, too bad that! Lose much?'

'All ma shares down the drain. Invested with Northern Rock. Sound local bank for years but the crash just wiped it out. That was my pension pot.'

Einar, sitting on the other side of Martin, spoke up.

'Norvik is the latest victim of the credit crisis that began in the American subprime mortgage market. Our town took out loans using future energy income as collateral. They had invested the money in a group with the promise that their investment would grow. Risks that should've been recognised were either ignored, or unappreciated.' Knutsen banged the table, looking around at the faces about him. 'The chief investigator for Norway's financial regulator told me they saw no terms about payments if the investment bottomed. Citigroup provided the information but they had signed the damn contact before the town received the copy. Can you believe the incompetency?'

Lesley, the Brit chimed in, 'You know there were queues outside the bank. First Northern Rock as Bob mentioned, then we saw other banks affected, including the Royal Bank of Scotland.'

The others seemed to have locked in to the conversation. Kim moved on her chair uncomfortably and tried to get Martin's attention. Betsy from Cincinnati added to the growing strength of feelings.

'So, it seems many of us have been stung by those crooks, the Lehman brothers. The financial institutions have made a lot of money while Cindy is fearful that her teachers' pension has been wiped out.' Her daughter nodded but remained quiet.

'That's not the half, did ya hear the police, fire service, highways patrol agency are all affected? The news is all over and the politicians are ripping at everyone. Ted Strickland for the Democrats is attacking John Kasich for earning a huge salary and bonuses from the Lehman brothers.'

'Yeah I know, Mom, Kilroy's a Democrat, and he's pushing the House Committee on Financial Services after a report found that Lehman tried to hide $50 billion in debt ahead of the collapse.'

Kim coughed, trying to attract attention away from the subject. She was all too aware of how Martin made his money, and with their move to the Hamptons and the holiday in South America they certainly had nothing to worry about, except their Charlotte. As far as Kim was concerned, she would trade it all in for Charlotte to be well again.

'I think David wants to show his slides. You know, the evening lecture?' she interjected.

'You know what I can't stomach, well, let me tell you. It's the fact they were all trading and moving imaginary money around. It's not just a tragedy but a scandal and it's affected the whole world.

Kim left Martin with the others, feeling bad that only a few listened to David's PowerPoint. Moths and giant insects crashed into his screen noisily now that dark had descended and the nocturnal insect world had come alive.

Martin regretted the late night as they entered the jungle the next day. They walked across a floor made of dying leaves, a heavy ingrained white natural fungus called micorhiza added to the different colours and textures. Birds sang cheerful songs as the canoes set out to reach a local Kichwa tribal village. Beautifully made cooking utensils and fishing traps constructed from palm tree leaves were laid out for the visitors. Then native weapons were demonstrated after they left the museum-like hut. One villager delighted in explaining the blowpipe.

'The dart is dipped in curare formed into a brown sticky resin that can cause paralysis in the victim. We make it into a ball of wool and it fits snuggly in this laminated tube 2.3 metres long.'

Bob commented, 'That's pretty amazing and look how accurate he was.' The dart sat firmly in the centre of a cardboard target pinned to a tree.

A wizened old man with bowlegs sat cross-legged, ignoring the band of tourists as they entered his thatched hut. This was the Shaman they had all come to see. His naked torso showed his coffee-coloured skin with somewhat over-large male breasts. Deep furrows in his forehead looked like a ploughed field. His rotten teeth were yellow-brown.

Kim squeezed Martin's arm. 'He must be over 100 years old. Do you think he'll be able to help us?' she said in a hushed tone. 'Martin, ask if he knows any medicine for arthritis,' jabbing him in the side.

'Er, fella, yes you, can I have a word?'

The agent, a local tribesman leaned toward Martin.

'Do you think your man here might know of any cures for arthritis?' Martin asked. The agent turned to the Shaman and started speaking rapidly in Kichwa. In turn, the Shaman moved his head and came forward. Bamboo-like teeth became more prominent as his discoloured lips receded in a fake smile.

'He says there are certain conditions this concoction can help.'

Kim was concentrating firmly on the discussion, unaware that the group had started to ease out of the hut.

'Does he mean how progressive or advanced the condition is?'

'No lady, he is talking about how much.'

David returned and could see the four figures deep in conversation. He had found his two missing tourists.

'You can't. Sorry Kim, sorry Martin, we simply cannot stop the tour for two people wanting a private consultation.' David seemed distressed at his awkward position. 'Tomorrow we're scheduled to return down the creek to find the salt licks. They're an amazing sight when the parrots come out.'

Martin's expression looked grim and Kim knew that look.

'Listen you little shit, I don't give a fuck about parrots. I want to talk to this medicine doctor so piss off and we'll find our way back.'

Martin was used to getting his own way. David looked offended as no doubt anyone would.

'Look Martin, I have a responsibility...'

'Okay, then how much to hold this party up a bit?'

'What do you mean, Martin, how much?'

'How much to get someone to take us back to the Shaman?'

'I don't know.'

'Well, friggin well find out, and fast, before we leave.'

One hundred dollars secured a boat, two paddlers and approved separation from the tour. Excited, Kim thought of the South American medicine that would help their daughter.

The money was a shake down for sure. Having done enough shady deals himself, Martin knew he was being conned.

The entrance to the Shaman's hut was narrow. Orange embers danced from a small wood fire as the warm air wafted through the doorway. The agent's words were spoken in good English, although his Spanish flattened some of the vowels.

'Sit and do not speak during the ceremony. I'll translate for you. Don't be alarmed by noises and raised voices, these are normal. The Shaman is sensitive to outside spirits and if you want this to work you must have complete trust.'

The Shaman used only Kichwa language. The thick leather blanket hanging from the door slapped closed, cutting off any external light. The fire flared as a powder was thrown onto a low burning fire by the leathery-skinned old man wearing his dirty loin cloth.

'Now before we begin, you must understand this is a contract.'

'What, you want me to sign a piece of paper in the dark?'

'No, you will not have to sign any paper, just agree. Your daughter WILL be cured. In return you have to pay the Kichwa tribe $100,000. I have the bank details written down so when you get home you can make the arrangements. Is this agreed?'

'You've got to be kidding me, son.'

'No, I am deadly serious. If you want your daughter to be well you will pay this sum to our tribe. This medicine is powerful and works.'

'So, what you're saying is you'll do all the voodoo stuff and we get to pay you when we get home stateside?'

'That's correct,' ignoring the stupid comment about Voodoo.

'We trust you.' Kim touched her husband's arm. 'Martin,' she said in a quiet voice. 'We agreed. Charlie's worth it.' Martin considered the arrangement. He could pay what he felt when he got home, so hell, agree now. What could they do about it once he had the protection of the USA?

The agent added, as if knowing what Martin was thinking. 'If you refuse to pay no harm will come to your daughter…'

Martin thought, 'Sucker!'

'But should you not honour our agreement then you personally will suffer the consequences.'

With the contract agreed verbally, the Shaman proceeded. He started to hum and wave his arms. After a minute he stopped and spoke through the agent, his grandson; a doctor who lived in Coca.

'Ayahuasca is a brew mixed from leaves and root bark. It forms the basis of the medicine.'

He did not explain the potent chemical effect the ayahuasca could have; and the fact that each brew varied. The monoaminooxidase inhibitors, when mixed with certain foods, could cause increased blood pressure.

The agent knew all of this and took precautions. He helped make the brew his grandfather was using. A dark brown viscous material was poured into a bowl and offered to Martin.

'But I thought this was to be taken by my daughter?'

'No, you must take it as your daughter lives so far away,' the agent explained. Martin doubted the medicine's effects and convinced himself it was mumbo jumbo. But the fact that his wife was so serious meant he had to play along.

'We are conducting this treatment through her direct blood ascendant.'

'Okay then, if you say so.' The taste was bitter and then sweet. Its syrupy mixture radiated warmly down his throat. His stomach received the mixture with some indignation as a sensation of air-filled expansion took place. 'Okay what now…'

The Shaman waved his Suru Panga (blow leaves) over Martin's head while chanting. He started to blow then made hawking noises from his stomach. His words slurred.

Martin looked around the space, and viewed everyone with the clarity of a powerful light beam. A smile appeared on his face but then disappeared as his breathing changed. He threw himself forwards involuntarily and vomited. No longer able to hear clearly, he could just make out Kim asking the agent what was happening. Martin remained outside the conversation.

'Is he all right? Should this happen? It looks as if he is in pain.'

'There's nothing to worry about, this is all quite normal. The ayahuasca will purge any worms.'

'But he's never had worms.'

Martin felt more strange sensations. The room darkened again and he mumbled. He saw his daughter walking normally, and behind her a dark figure closed in then went bright. The meaning was unclear. A smell developed in the room. He could not place it.

'Christ, he's shit himself,' Kim said, somewhat alarmed. 'I suppose that's to clear the worms as well?'

'The psychedelic effects of ayahuasca lead to great elation, fear, or illumination. Its purgative properties are considered important,' the agent said.

Martin slept for about thirty minutes then awoke refreshed. 'What happened? Oh Christ, I've shit myself!'

NEW YORK

Returning First Class from South America, two tired passengers deplaned at JFK. They reached the Hamptons in under two hours. Traffic was heavy. The Sagoponack Village home had a price tag valued at around six million. Martin also had an apartment in mid-centre Manhattan, not far from Central Park, which he used during the working week. A maid let them in and took care of their luggage. A young woman dressed in a neat blue suit came into the hall, face beaming.

'Hi Mom, Dad.'

Kim stared at her daughter. She stood upright, no crutches, no chair. Make-up gave her a youthful appearance and her hair had lost the wiry dull sheen. Light brown colours replaced her grey strands. Her hands were straight, with no deformities of the fingers or wrists. Her voice was soft, full of cheer. Her mouth opened without the pain that Kim recalled. Her words were clear. She wore matching blue shoes with a heel. There was no limp as she bounced on the balls of her feet with excitement, if not elation. She rushed into first her mother's arms, then hugged her father.

'How? When?' Kim stuttered, forgetting Martin's ordeal.

'I woke up two days ago and found I could walk. It's a miracle. Rachel couldn't believe it. I told her she didn't need to stay anymore.'

Normality returned to the Piscarro family home. Six months went by. South America was behind Martin, or so he thought. The day was warm and he took his lunch to the park. Standing in front of the Daniel Webster statue, he felt utter pride being an American, even if he did have Spanish blood in him somewhere. Wagner Cove was rustic and quiet, accessed by a small path. He sat on one of the two wooden benches then opened his case to retrieve a salmon-stuffed bagel with cream cheese. The voice behind startled him.

The agent looked very different. Gone were the loose clothes and unkempt hair, the dark beard growth. A man stood tall with a neat clean-shaven face, manicured hands. The cologne was notable but not overpowering.

'Jeeze, you scared me half to death.'

'Erick Valarezo, Mr Piscarro. Do you recall me?' Valarezo let his question sink in. 'Let me get to the point, our contract. The agreed price was $100,000 and should have been paid into our bank account. We have only received $10,000. Can I ask what has happened to the other $90,000?'

'Well, son...'

'Please don't call me your son, I am DOCTOR Valarezo.'

'Sorry, as I was explaining, Dr Valarezo, I paid what I thought was a fair price, and that was somewhat over the top if you ask me.'

'This is not the point, we had an agreement. A contract which you verbally acceded to after we had informed you of all the relevant information. Is your daughter not cured?'

'Yes, she is, but our doctors have helped her and I cannot see how taking medicine myself could have influenced this. To be honest, Valarezo, I think you have rather played me and you should think yourself lucky that you have $10,000 at all.'

'Mr Piscarro, let me assure you that your daughter would never have been cured by conventional means. She had a severe form of arthritis and could have died from dislocation of the spine during routine dental treatment.'

'How could you possibly know this, you charlatan?'

'Mr Piscarro, this is my only warning. I implore you to heed this. The Shaman cannot reverse a breach in the contract. You have 24 hours left.'

'Look Valarezo, this is the United States of America and we have laws here, not like your backward country that relies on the US to support its banking. You would be wise to heed my words and desist from putting unreasonable pressure on me. Scientifically, and you should know this as a doctor, the chance of anyone helping my daughter from 4000 miles away is unbelievable.'

'My grandfather just wanted to warn you. Personally, it matters little to me.'

Martin watched the tall man disappear, as he bit into his bagel.

Martin stayed over in his New York apartment rather than travelling back to the Hamptons. It had been two days of meetings and he felt exhausted. After watching an old film, Martin headed for his room. Turning the adjustable ceiling lights down, he switched on the built-in CD player. He quickly called Kim to say goodnight then played some soft music while he readied for bed.

Funny man that Valarezo. Did he really think I would pay the full amount? He had decided not to tell Kim. He knew she would be annoyed. You had to be careful with money, he mused to himself. Any irony was lost. So many had suffered. The pain caused by one click on the keyboard had been disproportionate.

The greed of a few men had exerted pain across the globe. It soon became apparent that no one was held accountable. On the other hand, suppose a different pain hit a single person, encapsulating all the disease symptoms over his lifetime at once? The hurt from a cut magnified by a hundred cuts and bruises. Two hundred headaches. Fever accumulated from colds and flu. The pain from dozens of injections, including dental work. An aggregated pain score would soon make matters very different. Humans could bear the pain, and as Charlotte had found, chronic pain was something you could just about cope with, at a cost. Acute pain would be very different and surely you would faint. But Martin did not have even the faintest knowledge of medical matters, and he was unaware, at least until that moment, of the consequences of accumulated pain.

He climbed into bed and shut his eyes. After an hour, unable to sleep he suddenly sat bolt upright. Intense discomfort hit him.

As we grow older, a doctor once said,

'*The pain associated with minor injuries, strains, increasing headaches hurts, BUT we just adapt over time. We get used to it. Accustomisation is part of the coping mechanism. A painkiller soon settles the hurt we feel, and better painkillers keep pain under control. But imagine accelerated pain. The build-up normally arriving gently over time and usually tolerated, all hitting us at once. Fifty years of accumulated discomfort would be enough to kill you.'*

… this was the pain that now hit Martin. His back arched. His arms stretched upwards involuntarily. Heat tore into his joints and spasm twisted his spine, radiating down to his hands and feet, through his shoulders, elbows, legs and knees. Both feet went into clonus, pointing downwards as if performing en pointe. His lips stretched back, his gums exposed his teeth and his jaw locked tight. Saliva flecked with blood dribbled out of his mouth where his teeth caught his tongue. Tears streamed from his eyes and his nose oozed as his mucous membranes discharged. Every nerve fibre was hyperactive, a flood of chemicals producing a river of inflammation and cascaded, like the outflow from a volcano bleeding red lava down its steep slopes. Cells usually arranged in their normal numerical distribution erupted without any sense of homeostatic control. Such physiological changes should never occur, and certainly not altogether. His ankles swelled and his heart raced, tightening his chest. Suddenly the tiny buds deep in his lungs, hanging from the branches like grapes, failed to exchange waste gases for oxygen. Deep purple replaced his healthy pink skin. Vessels in his eyes popped, stealing their natural colour, then his eyes bulged as if squeezed from his head

As his eyeballs protruded, the rictus on his face prevented the scream he tried to make. In the twenty seconds since the first series of pains hit, he could not turn his head to retrieve the phone. Spasm after spasm fired like a machine gun spanning across a battlefield. The arch in his lower back burned now locked in full extension while sweat poured out of him. His hands dripped with sweat and his bladder lost control so urine soaked the bed. The content that had settled in the lower portions of the bowel were no longer retained and dribbled from his now-relaxed sphincter. He was by now only aware of these intense, extreme noxious stimulations preventing him from responding to anything. Humanity had left him as he took a thousand pains. Darkness crept closer and light burst into the room, but Martin Piscarro was already dead.

Eddie Durran stared at the body twelve hours later, having been called to the scene. He sighed, chalking it up to yet another suicide.

The medical examiner had been shocked by his latest customer. The raw skin had split in places. Few joints were spared. The ME started the process; dissecting, photographing, measuring and weighing organs and his bodily contents sent for closer examination under the microscope. Their results suggested a thousand diseases and pathologies.

Peter Elfin sat at the kitchen table with a cup of strong black coffee. He looked intently at page three of the *New York Times*:

Death of Man. Mysterious Circumstances?

FINANCIER MARTIN PISCARRO WAS FOUND DEAD YESTERDAY IN HIS APARTMENT NEAR CENTRAL PARK, SAID FBI SPOKESMAN, BERNIE ELDEFLOWER. PISCARRO WORKED WITH ANOTHER CEO FOR THE ATLAS FINANCIAL CORPORATION AND EARNED $300 MILLION IN SALARY AND OTHER INCOME DURING THE HOUSING BUBBLE. HE UNLOADED $120 MILLION IN HIS STOCK OPTIONS BEFORE THE COMPANY'S SHARE PRICE COLLAPSED.

SHAREHOLDERS TOOK THE HIT. HIS PARTNER ANZILLO SETTLED WITH THE SEC FOR SECURITIES FRAUD AND INSIDER TRADING, PAYING $67.5 MILLION IN FINES. AT THE TIME OF HIS DEATH, PISCARRO WAS UNDER INVESTIGATION.

'Vengeance is a dish best served cold,' Peter muttered. His wife appeared unsure at the meaning but noted satisfaction on his face.

EPILOGUE

ECUADOR, SOUTH AMERICA

Valarezo had returned to his ancestral tribal home, and was back in loose-fitting clothes. 'Hello David, how are you?'

His brother hugged him and they both sat down to drink with their grandfather.

The Shaman looked at both grandsons through narrow slits from his grizzled dark brown face and chuckled. Wearing a light-coloured safari suit, he appeared anything other than the wizened old man. He had removed the false teeth and smiled with clean, white, healthy ones. His face seemed younger now, devoid of makeup. He still hawked and spat from habit. Erick didn't mind, he loved the wise old man who had made so many things possible. His community came first.

'The girl will be spared but will be sterile, the last of her family line, but at least she will live to be old,' his voice clear and modulated.

'Did Mr Piscarro not think we knew his real name? Piscarro is a derivation of Pizarro.'

THE TOURIST CAMP BY THE LAKE

David stood in front of his audience of tourists. His projector whirred, the light attracting mosquitoes and insects of all sizes.

'The Amazon was re-discovered by the Spanish and so named after the Aztecs sent them on a wild goose chase … the brutality of their generals, in particular, General Francisco Pizarro Gonzalez, one of the most hated Spaniards ever to set sail and infamous to the Kichwa tribe… Pizarro was stabbed by a young Kichwa warrior in 1541 called Valarezo. In 1977 Pizarro's head was located in Peru. It had been hacked off and buried separately from the torso.'

Of course David could not tell the story until now. The contract concluded to the tribe's satisfaction.

Author's Note

A change of scenery takes us up the River Napo and an eco-lodge in Ecuador. I wanted to try to create the wonderment of the so-called jungle and a desire to find a cure for Charlotte. Of course rheumatoid arthritis cannot be cured by an Amazonian potion but my memories of the Shaman in his chocolate leathery skin are vivid.

All the helpful information came from an authentic guide called David. The period of my trip to South America occurred around the time of the financial crash. Many suffered and the narrative tried to highlight some of the costs borne during this period, which Officer Durran observed. Of course those tales of woe did not just occur in the USA where our story starts.

The twist in the tale seemed appropriate as the Spanish, like so many Europeans, including the British, French, Portuguese and Dutch brought untold misery on peoples around the world. The tale about General Francisco Pizarro being stabbed by a young Kichwa warrior in 1541 called Valarezo is true.

BRODIE'S DECEPTION

LONDON, British Parliament, July 1915

Mr O'Grady asked the Minister of Munitions whether the firm of Thomas Firth and Sons, Sheffield, is engaged in war work... and whether, in view of the appeals being made for skilled workmen for munitions work, he will make inquiries into this matter.

Dr Christopher Addison: 'I am making inquiries into the point raised by my hon. friend and will communicate with him as to the result.'

Hansard Parliamentary record

FRANCE, September 1915

Standing on a duckboard above the drainage sump where
water and soft mud gathered, a corporal eyed the soldier
above while smoking an Ogden's cigarette. An orange
flare shot across no man's land, illuminating the gap
between the German forces and the British. The
landscape was peppered with coils of vicious barbed
wire.

Staring back at the British trench, a man dressed in
drab grey moved slightly to release the ache from his
upper thigh. He wore a soft hat, but was cleverly hidden
amongst some debris. Only someone with an
experienced eye would have made out the muzzle of his
Gewehr 98 Mauser rifle. He took care not to knock the
offset Otto Bock scope, the tool of his trade.

Now dark, there was little opportunity to use the rifle
unless someone was stupid enough to draw light
themselves. He was well practised and a patient man.
This characteristic made him deadly but with due respect
for an unseen enemy, his caution also kept him alive. He
could wait. There would soon be an opportunity as the
sun would rise and someone would be careless. His tally
of British Tommies had been impressive these last few
weeks. Khaki trophies were mounting.

THREE WEEKS EARLIER

Major Robert Burnett stooped in the confined space of
the small room. He was a Cambridge graduate, but his
student days were long past.

The men around him stood a head shorter. He moved
behind Colonel Fleming to find a better position. In the
short space, his limp was imperceptible, but the cold and
damp reminded him of the injury some sixteen years

ago. Another time, another war and another conflict with humanity.

The Colonel addressed two soldiers, one a sergeant, the other a lieutenant both standing in front of his makeshift desk. Captain Chambers, Fleming's adjutant, stood close by the Colonel's shoulder, looking serious. As Fleming's right hand man, the Colonel leaned on Chambers heavily for the endless administration required. Fleming had constantly told him, 'You are indispensable, Chambers.'

Addressing the senior of the two men, Fleming said, 'Lieutenant Pierce, you're to return to England post haste with Sergeant Miller. Captain Chambers will supply you with anything you need. This is of the utmost urgency. You will leave immediately. Passes have been arranged.'

Fleming outlined the task and unshrouded some of the mystery for Pierce and Miller. Burnett remained quiet in the background while the two lower rankers were receiving their instructions. Chambers added the occasional comment with a nod and a 'quite so' from his commander.

Major General Hart's son had been killed two days earlier. Investigations had shown his helmet had been defective. The new helmets were supposed to be a better design than those used by the French, and offered better shrapnel protection. An artillery barrage had burst across the forward trenches. Those with the new Brodie helmet had fared better against the indiscriminate fragments, but a number, including General Hart's son, were fatally wounded.

'The quarter-master informed us that some, but not all, helmets were defective,' Fleming informed Pierce and Miller. 'Your task, Lieutenant, is to find the source and eliminate those perpetrators who for self-gain have endangered the lives of their own countrymen. I want them found and brought back and charged with treason.'

Chambers supplied Pierce and Miller with passes. They would use the French train to the coast and take a ship for the short passage back to England to start their quest. As they were preparing to leave, the tall figure of Staff Officer Burnett appeared. This time his limp was more pronounced.

'Miller, a word?'

'Yes sir. Excuse me, Lieutenant,' Sam said to Pierce.

'Sam, how are you? Haven't seen you for some time.'

'No sir. Spent some months out in Gallipoli and returned to Blighty with the shits! Poor buggers are still out there, but thanks for assigning me here. Stomach still plays up but it's a lot better without the heat and contaminated water.'

'Yes quite. I understand...'

Burnett had connections with the Miller family. Sam Miller's father, Richard, had been close friends of Robert Burnett and had served Her Majesty's forces in the Boer War. He had saved Burnett's life on more than one occasion. Richard had been a loyal man who had sadly been killed some years earlier. Burnett had vowed to do what he could for his family.

'Look, we have a situation. There's a spy at work and we need to flush him out. How far it goes down the line we don't know yet, but we are trying to unravel the mystery. Protect the Lieutenant, he's trustworthy, but no-one else. Suspect everyone, and I mean everyone. I want you guarding his back, but let him lead. I know you have more experience than some of these young officers. Sadly it seems many of them last only weeks out here. Look, I want you to use your own intuition. We need to bring those responsible back for judgement, as I need to interrogate them.'

Burnett was not just an ordinary staff officer, but an acting colonel on a major's pay. As an intelligence officer, he was fluent in Afrikaans, French, German and Dutch. He was an exceptional shot, having originally been brought up by a Boer family with Dutch and French ancestry. But his shooting didn't compare to Sam who could take the wing off a bumble bee at 15 yards. Before Burnett limped off, he said, 'Oh yes, I had better tell you. This mission is "top secret" and off the books. General Hart denies all knowledge. You'll be out of uniform once back home, although Lieutenant Pierce is expected to wear the King's uniform.' With that he saluted the sergeant and walked away with his unusual gait.

ENGLAND, Sheffield.

Sam had tried to make out the substance of the mission and wondered how much he could talk about it to his Lieutenant. Both had worked together since Sam had returned to active duty. As partners, they undertook the murderous work of the sniper. Out of earshot, the senior officer and NCO used first names.

'Well Sam, we've been through a few scrapes so far, but this mission is a bit different.'

'Any chance of seeing family this trip?' Sam asked.

'I doubt it, as we only have a few days to deal with the problem.'

Burnett had also briefed Edward (Ted) Pierce earlier. The need-to-know attitude prevailed as Burnett knew that walls had ears. He suggested they start with one of the larger supply firms and act as workers, listen and find out anything they could. The use of the local constabulary was not desirable, but Pierce had to make that call.

Having reached Sheffield in the north of England by train, their passage so far had been smooth. Sam was now dressed in civvies. Both had agreed that he needed his uniform for the journey or he would have been questioned for not enlisting. There was also the added risk of being given a white feather, the emblem of cowardice.

His uniform was now packed away so he wore the typical garb of one of the locals heading to the factory, complete with olive green and mustard-coloured jacket, short collarless striped shirt, cloth cap, and corduroy trousers held up with a thick leather belt. Ted had also changed for this part of the role, as they tried to see if jobs were available. His attire looked less creased and more upmarket. Chambers, true to his word, had plied them with passes and papers. He had also given them a backstory which he assured would hold up if checked. Ted could pass as a draughtsman and Sam a regular worker. Sam had had a bit of help from his brother who specialised in working with metal and engineering design. He knew he could pass off as a general jobsworth.

It felt strange to both men being out of uniform. Side by side they made their way to Windsor Street. A light rain had started shortly after they had left their digs. Even there, Chambers seemed to have opened doors, and both were welcomed without questions being asked. Their hobnail boots made a sound of metal on the uneven pavement running down one side of the River Don. They headed into the Norfolk works and joined a queue, appearing to be signing up separately.

Stan Bassett, the senior manager, was tall, with closely-cropped ginger hair and a small moustache. He kept this gingery growth well trimmed, unlike some who looked like walruses. His face was pock marked and he had a scowl written all over. He didn't look like manager material and his solid frame appeared better built for rough work. He was similarly attired to Sam, wearing a worn jacket and corduroy trousers and a belt, rather than a suit. A packet of Ogden's Guinea Gold cigarettes lay on the foreman's desk. He picked up the packet, placed a cigarette in his mouth and lit the end.

'So what can you all do?' The match struck first time, leaping into a yellow flare, allowing him to complete the task of lighting the tobacco. He sucked in deeply, enjoying the infusion of smoke inhaled into his lungs. 'Got a secret weapon against the fuckin' Zeppelins eh?' He chuckled at his joke. 'Bastards are having another go at London. God help us if they get up here 'cos this is where the bleeding action is.'

'You first,' he said staring at an older man wearing a peaked cap. The man took his cap off and held it at waist height. His hair extended to the sides, while for the most part he was bald.

'A bit old aren't you, Grandpa?' Bassett accused.

The man turned out to be a miner, but Bassett was not particular and said okay sign on.

Sam stared at the wall. A poster showed Kaiser Wilhelm in a goal being winded by a football. The ball was in the colours of the Union Flag, the red, white and blue making the pattern well known the world over. Many a game had been given away when an enemy had used the flag, being unaware that it was not symmetrical and had flown it the wrong way up.

All schoolboys knew the unique flag comprised of the nations of Scotland, Ireland and England. The important bit was getting the coloured crosses right. Wales didn't get a look in as the country had become part of England centuries earlier and had a dubious status.

Glancing at the poster, Sam noticed the foot appeared at one edge, having kicked the ball at the aristocratic German leader. The simple caption was one word.

'GOAL!' If only that was true, thought Sam, who had been on two different war fronts. One within the Ottoman Empire on the far edge of Europe, and one in Northern France. Neither front gave the impression that Britain was winning, but without doubt the war affected the world. They had said it would all be over by Christmas 1914, but here they all were more than a year on.

'Right, draftsman you say? Let's see,' Bassett said as he examined the paperwork Ted Pierce had offered up. He sucked in some more of the cigarette. Ash darted upwards and he closed his eye momentarily.

'All right, we'll set you up copying to start with. Bosses are always after plans to send to the Ministry. 7/6 a week is the starting pay. And you son... Bit of a dogs body aren't you?' Clearly Stan was unimpressed with Sam's credentials. 'Okay you can go to the sheds. We're doing a spray job on them new tin bowlers. You can make yourself useful there.'

Sam looked up at Ted and their eyes connected, pleased that one of them would be placed in the right section. This had always been a gamble. If that had failed they would have followed the men from the factory when they left work at the end of the day. Locating their drinking hole was the back-up plan. This was almost too good to be true.

'You can both start right away. We've got a big order on...' The foreman looked at Sam's paperwork. 'Wallace – that's Wally right?'

'Yes sir, Mr Bassett, thank you, sir.'

'Right, I'll get someone to take you to your job sections. We work in shifts so you're lucky as yours will finish early today.'

Sam looked at the large open space. Helmets were hanging down from a wooden frame with horizontal bars which had been dipped in drab olive green. He pushed the heavy wooden trolley on wheels up a ramp into the drying oven as he had been shown.

'Ey up young lad, ow yer doing there?' an old hand commented.

'Fine thanks, mate, all good. You got many working here now?'

'Some. Lost a few to the King's shilling 'cos you know the pressure's on. Young'uns think they ought to do their bit, you know. Me, I'm too old. Any road, did my bit in the last war.'

'What? You fought in Africa against the Boers?'

'Yeah sure did, that was until we got holed up in Kimberley with that ponce Rhodes for five months. He was forever giving orders and him no military man. Yeah we got out in the end, but nearly starved to death. Ate all the bloody horses. Yeah, reckon I've done my bit for country and the Queen, well that's when we had a Queen. Now Georgie boy's there. 'Im and that Kaiser geezer. They're related did you know that?'

Sam knew all of this well. His father Richard had fought in South Africa in 1899 but had also seen the bad side of an army fighting innocent women and children in the concentration camps. His grandmother had drilled into him about fairness and fights. The old timer invited Sam for a drink after work and this seemed a good idea. He could get a pie and chips down at the Old Smithy public house. He would meet up with Ted later and share anything he found out.

The old timer took Sam to the Old Smithy as planned after work. While there was profit in this meeting, he had difficulty standing up after the drinking session. Trying to hide his sensitivity to alcohol was not easy, despite the fact that the beer had been watered down. It had taken him some years to recover from his first incident with alcohol. This had happened when a sailor in the British Navy at Plymouth had bought him his first drink and he had passed out. After that he'd found himself in the navy!

'You look worse for wear, Sam. Thought you avoided the drink?' Ted commented.

'I did my best, but the only way to loosen tongues was to join in.'

'How did you do it then, I mean not get rat arsed?'

'I spilled a lot of beer!'

'So what did you learn?'

'Well apart from men enlisting and thinning out the work force they reckon they'll be recruiting women next.'

'Forget the women. What about the men?'

'I was getting to that. Two men left back end of the year and did not enlist but the real story was that some equipment went missing. They couldn't pin it on them and they moved to Leeds and got employment there.'

'Go on...'

'One of the workers has a brother-in-law and he told his sister, the worker's wife, that someone was after the equipment. Get this. The equipment was a machine for pressing metal and not only that, but it was also designed for the new helmet.'

'Young Sam, you did well. All we need is a name and an address.'

It was a joke as the Lieutenant, although a full officer and not a subaltern, was younger than Sam by one year. Sam had seen far more action than the Lieutenant.

'Right,' said Ted, 'I reckon we need to break in and get the records for these men. Any idea what they might have been called?'

'Only one name came up – Albert Ryan,' Sam said.

Both men turned up for work as normal the next day. Ted was asked to take some plans to one of the offices and found himself passing a room near to where he and Sam had been recruited the day before. The weathered wooden unit had a number of drawers with brass knobs. He looked hopefully at the filing cabinet, which had the potential to yield the information he was after. He walked in and saw a young woman tapping away on a typewriter.

'Can I help you sir?' she asked. He noticed that her accent was not from the north of England.

'Sorry to bother you, Miss. I was wanting to check up on a man who might be able to help me out with these plans.'

This was the best he could do, thinking on his feet. Naively he had not expected to meet anyone while he searched. He knew he was a little off course. The sound of laughter suggested Stan was back in his office.

'I could look for you if you want... you are?'

'Er, Thomas, Tom Egerton,' he replied, coming up with one of his fellow officer's names.

'Right Tom, what's 'is name then?' the young woman asked.

'Albert Ryan, he left a few months ago and went to Leeds.'

'Ackers, Adelyn, Aggerton, Ahearne, Akton...'

'I think you could try under the surname, Miss. It is Miss isn't it...?'

'Jean, you can call me Jean. Sorry, don't know what I was thinking... Ah yes, here I've got a Ryan. Actually I've got two Ryans. One lives here in Sheffield, the other says no known address.'

Laughter increased and Stan Bassett walked in. His smile disappeared as he recognised Ted. 'Egerton you're not supposed to be here. What are you doing?'

Ted had to think fast again, as the last thing he wanted was to be found out or get Jean into trouble.

'Sorry Mr Bassett, it's all rather embarrassing. I sort of shouldn't say as I don't want to insult the kind lady here.'

'What, Jean? Ha, don't worry about her she's just a hireling. Now come on, what is it? Make it good or you'll be out this very moment with a cuff around the ear.'

Ted bridled at the insult to Jean and tried to sound genuine. 'Erm, I wanted to ask Jean out. I'm sorry, Jean, I've been so forward like this but I'm a passionate man and cannot help myself when it comes to a good-looking woman.'

'Pah, you young men only think of one thing. Go on, get out of here before I box your ears just for fun.'

Jean blushed as Ted left. She looked at Bassett, who did not look pleased at all. Once Ted had disappeared, he turned back to Jean and backhanded her so she fell against the table.

'You stupid bitch, what was he looking for? Tell me or I'll give you a thrashing.'

Tears stung her eyes as she tried to face down the bully who stood a good foot taller.

'S'pose you beat all women do you if you don't get your way? You're a bloody rotten coward, that's what you are, a bloody rotten coward,' she said through her sobs.

Ted and Sam were walking back to their digs after the day's shift. The light was still bright enough to make out a woman crying on a wooden bench amongst a small, well-kept area with a few trees and flower beds. 'Jean, is that you?' Ted asked.

She looked up. The right side of her face was bruised, her eyes red from crying.

'What on earth happened here?' He had to wait several minutes for an answer while she sobbed uncontrollably.

'The bastard hit me after you left and wanted to know what you was after. Sorry Tom, I had to tell him. He twisted my arm and was going to break my nose. A girl's got her looks you know after all...'

'So, the snivelling little coward now knows what we're about? We'd better break in and get that card for the address you mentioned,' Sam spoke for the first time.

Jean sniffed. 'No need, I made a copy here.'

'That's fantastic and so thoughtful, Jean,' realising that he had actually made his thoughts known to a stranger. 'I am so sorry to have put you through this.' Ted asked sympathetically hoping that he could commit her to their secret plans.

He really liked Jean, although she was a bit below his ranks. Mummy and Daddy were keen for him to marry the local vicar's daughter, Sylvia. This was what he planned to do as soon as the war was over. Unlike Sam who came from the West Country, Ted had been brought up around Oxford and had attended one year at the university studying chemistry. The class system was very much alive in England.

'I dunno, he might, but I'm right scared I have to tell you.'

Sam recognised the London accent and wondered what had brought her up to Sheffield. He decided not to ask anything further as he didn't want to put Jean's life in danger.

The address on the paper for Albert Ryan was 73 Scott Road, around Pittsmoor. The landlady said it would take around ten minutes via Attercliffe Road. Sam and Ted wondered what they would find. The next morning, they set off early and hid behind a nearby wall so they weren't seen. They waited two hours and then approached the house as no-one was coming or going. An elderly woman answered the door. She wore a floral dress and had the largest bustline Sam had ever seen on a woman. He wondered if they could be used as airships!

'Is Mr Ryan in please?' Ted asked, noticing Sam seemed to be close to breaking out with laughter.

'No he'll be out presently as he's at work,' the lady with the large bust said. 'Anyway, who wants to know?'

'Where would that be then?' Ted ignored the question. 'We might be able to catch up with him.'

She confirmed that Ryan worked at a nearby factory, but failed to say where.

'It's difficult to say, love, but you could try seven o'clock tonight, when he's back from work. Anyway, Mr Ryan won't be wanting me to give out his details to any old sod,' she replied.

'Thank you, we will come back later then,' said Ted

'What do you reckon? Not helpful but not unhelpful?' Sam responded.

'Well I'd hardly call her helpful. Why not tell us where he works? Is she protecting him?'

'If you ask me, she was evasive,' Sam said.

'I agree, but then she invited us to call back, which might under usual circumstances be a normal response,' Ted replied.

'Well I'm not happy just to turn up. This bloke might be up to his eyeballs in it! I don't want an unwelcoming reception party.'

'I'm sure it won't come to that, Sam.'

'Nevertheless, when we come back I'll climb over the back if you do the front.'

Ted agreed to this suggestion and then added as an afterthought, 'So what was the smiling about then, Sam?'

Sam told him...

The light was ebbing on their return to Scott Road that evening. Sam insisted the two of them split up and found his way around the back of the terraced properties. Ted took the front as before.

Sam was pleased they had surveyed the lie of the land earlier which meant they knew how to make a quick getaway if it was required. They had turned up at work on a later shift so no suspicions had been aroused. There was no sign of Jean or Bassett when they'd arrived to clock on. Getting back to Pittsmoor created no difficulty but they had had no time to eat.

Sam found a wall and could see this was the back of number 73. The top of the wall was rounded, making it slightly more difficult to achieve a hand purchase. And then there was the slimy patina that lay across the top, causing his hands to slip. After heaving his body up with some effort he dropped down the other side, flexing his knees to deaden the sound and looked around for somewhere to discharge the green mess and seagull guano from his hands. His Lee-Enfield had been carefully lowered ahead of his jump, the stock resting on the ground. He cursed - 'Bloody birds,' he said thinking of his seaside home in Devon and the mess they made.

He unfastened his Lee-Enfield rifle. Slipping off the canvas case, and then ensured a .303 bullet was slid into the chamber. The bolt mechanism worked smoothly and the brass cartridge and bullet clicked into place. Finding a privy, common to all properties on the land, he checked to see if there were any tell-tale feet inside. The doors were short and went down no further than the tops of the ankle. Seeing no evidence of human occupation, he opened the door and looked inside. A wooden bench, a hole and sheets of newspaper.

Meanwhile, Ted knocked at the front. The heavy knocker hammered against a brass plate, announcing his arrival. The lady appeared again in the same dress and Ted could not fail to notice what Sam had described earlier. Indeed her chest was a size to behold, unlike those of Sylvia, his fiancée, with her slender frame. The woman showed him into the first room, and standing there was the tall figure of Stan Bassett, not Albert Ryan. By the look on his face he had been expecting Ted. Lieutenant Piece realised they had been set up, but how, he was unsure.

'So, reckon you aren't after Miss Jean Wells but after Mr Ryan. You're going to be disappointed.'

Ted looked shocked at Bassett's change of demeanour. His mind churned over, wondering just how much danger he was now in. Seeing Ted confused, Bassett carried on, giving the impression of being excited at catching this man out.

'Mr Ryan is in yonder Burngreave Graveyard. He found out a bit too much, you see, so we had to deal with him. Well...' and Bassett started to laugh then, 'that was after we got him to shift the stuff from the Norfolk works. Sort of implicated him, didn't it. We promised him a load of dosh. Of course we had no intention of paying him.'

'And I suppose the other Mr Ryan doesn't exist then?' Ted said.

'Of course not. Do you think we're stupid? You, young fellow, have just bitten off more than you can chew. Was that other fellow with you as well? What's his name, Wally? Ha, thought you could fool old Stan Bassett.'

'No, never seen him before,' Ted said.

'Well that may be true or not seeing as both of you turned up together. I reckon you're lying. Shame that whore Jean didn't come in as we would have worked her over.'

'WE?'

'Oh yes, meet my partner, Joss.'

Joss was much smaller than Bassett, but broad, with an intimidating bull neck which gave him a fierce, solid no nonsense appearance. Joss being present was of course no accident. Sam had been right all along, and he could have kicked himself for being so stupid. Thank the stars that Sam was not with him presently, but where on earth was the young marksman?

'We'll deal with Jean after we've sorted you out.'

Ted realised all of this information had been given freely as he was not going to be able to tell anyone his suspicions. His contact with the Colonel's adjutant Captain Chambers would arrive too late. Chambers had taken a train to Leeds and was starting his own investigations there with another sergeant.

To make a point, Bull Neck was holding a .38 Webley service revolver to Ted's head. Ted knew at this range he could not jump two people.

'Out the back, mate, we'll make this quick. Thanks Ma, you did good.'

That cleared up who the airship lady was. 'That's all right, son, don't want these bastards poking their noses in where it's not wanted,' she replied.

Ted was surprised at Ma's tone. He was pushed through into the scullery, the hexagonal muzzle of the .38 pistol dug painfully into his back.

Ma seemed to keep the scullery neat and tidy. The latch on the back door lifted and he was pushed outside. The light had faded fast, and without a full moon he wondered if he could make for the wall that Sam had navigated half an hour earlier. Ted hoped that Sam was not far away because he reckoned he didn't have long to live. The two men followed cautiously, expecting a second man but there wasn't anyone around.

Ted was feeling as scared as he had the first time he'd led a raiding party into the enemy trenches. He could see the end coming. Joss lifted the gun to his head. Bassett chuckled, 'Any last requests?'

'Yes, if I'm to die, tell me what happened to the machinery. Clearly no-one could remove such a heavy piece of gear without inside help. And, you do realise it's unpatriotic to sell defective gear to the army? Your little game has cost British soldiers their lives.'

Ted had raised his voice a decibel or two and just hoped Sam had not bunked off.

Bassett seemed in no hurry and held some pride in revealing his careful plans and entrepreneurship.

'Well you see, son, first of all I don't care. Second, I reckon I should be paid properly like some of those toffs.' He thought a bit and said, 'A bit like you. I knew that you're no draughtsman Lieutenant Edward Pierce, and that your accomplice is Sergeant Sam Miller.'

Ted's mouth dropped open: 'How the hell do you know that?'

And so Bassett revealed everything, leaving Ted's jaw wide at these revelations.

'We've got a nice little earner going and no-one's going to stop it, least of all Her bleeding Majesty's army. Kill the bastard, Joss, he's not worth anymore discussion.'

Joss's finger cocked back the hammer so it made an audible click. He loved this bit because it made his victims crap themselves at the last sound they would ever hear.

The .303 bullet was capable of passing through a sizable brick up to nine inches thick or solid oak up to 38 inches. Joss's head exploded out the back so splatter flashed up the wall like wet red paint, along with the odd bit of bone. Bassett never even heard the next bullet enter the chamber as Sam brought the lever back in one fluid movement. Ted looked at Bassett, who now looked worried. The fist was a reflex built up from anger and fright, and impacted with sufficient power to break Bassett's nose. He fell to his knees in pain. Ted shook his hand with the after pain of the punch.

Ma suddenly appeared holding a shotgun, bringing it up to meet Ted's chest. Sam fired again, reshaping her airships and forcing her back through the door with the impact of the projectile. She was dead by the time she hit the floor. Sam kicked open the privy door. Another bullet was in the chamber and ready to fire.

'Christ old chum, I thought I was a goner!' Ted said with relief.

'Well, I'm bloody glad I'm out of that privy. It stank worse than a cow's milking shed in summer,' Sam replied with a smirk on his face.

Bassett was looking at the torn, blood-covered chest of his mother. She lay with her legs at an awkward angle, straddled across the back door entrance, her skirt riding high, showing her bloomers. The two dead bodies were stowed in the scullery and Bassett was forced to sit on a chair. Ted now held Joss's Webley while Sam held the Enfield at the ready.

'We can do this the hard way or the easy way. Where's the factory and how many are involved in this caper?' Ted barked.

Bassett held a bloody rag to his nose. He knew the game was up.

*****

Like a western written into countless stories, Sam and Ted could so easily have waded in and shot everyone in the workshop with smoking guns.

The small workshop was part of a farm a few miles out of Sheffield. They had been aided by Bassett's willingness to give up the information in order to avoid a bullet. He realised his opponents were more than willing to use force. After all, as Jean had said, he was a dirty, rotten coward.

Most of the material had been stolen from the Norfolk works piece by piece. The helmets looked realistic from a distance but were made with cork and fibre like the old pith helmets in the Boer war. The difference was that Bassett's workforce had made a thin covering of metal over the cork-fibre, giving the appearance and sound of a quality metal helmet. While this would offer a modest amount of protection, compared to the new Brodie helmet being launched for the trenches, the lookalikes would split open like a melon when in contact with exploding shrapnel.

Poor General Hart's son was one of a number of soldiers who had died in this manner. Hart was not a man to let matters lie. His only son was now in a mass grave in France and someone had to pay. Robert Burnett had been brought in to find out what was happening. As an intelligencer, he was sharp but Burnett was not after the false helmet industry, no, he was after larger fish. His trust in Sam was complete and it was Burnett who had advised Hart, not Fleming, to bring Sam in. The police moved in with Lieutenant Pierce now in full uniform. Bassett would end up heading for the gallows.

The lone sniper sat at some height above the workshop on a hill overlooking the farm offering an excellent view. He took off his thin rimmed glasses and cleaned the lens with a fresh handkerchief. His Lee-Enfield was equipped with a German-made Otto Bock telescopic sight positioned off centre, instead of the P.P.Cos (Periscopic Prism Company) scope used by the British.

The sniper pulled back the lever so a .303 bullet entered the firing chamber. The cross hairs, or reticule, focused on Ted first as he spoke to a group of men. His finger resting on the trigger took up the pressure when suddenly he felt the pressure from the muzzle of a rifle press hard against his neck.

'If that finger is not away from that trigger in seconds your head will have a different shape.'

Captain Ross Chambers put the gun down and slowly rose from his crouched position.

'Not an easy shot to make, Captain, given the cross wind.'

'I reckon I could have made it, Sergeant Miller. So how did you find me?'

FRANCE. September 1915.

Light grew slowly as dawn broke through the darkness. The man with the moustache and grey felt cap saw the landscape come into focus. He pushed the stiffness in his limbs out of his mind. The Mauser rifle was an extension of his upper torso.

Across the gap called no man's land, deformed stumps curled like stalagmites across the barren terrain punctuated by craters. He could see steam emitting from the British Trench only a short distance away. Barbed wire criss-crossed the gap between the two armies strung out across Northern France and Belgium. Having reached a stalemate, it was now a waiting game.

The khaki figure leaned against the forwardmost part of the trench system. This was called an SAP, and protection came from bags piled on top of one another like a loose brick wall. The sand could stop even the most powerful bullet in its tracks, hence why they were so important as part of the trench system. The lone figure seemed to shiver, an Ogden cigarette dangled from his nervous lips care of the man standing below on a duck board. The wooden slats sat above a drainage sump where water and soft mud gathered keeping the corporal dry. The NCO eyed the soldier above guarding him with distain. The soldier sucked on the proffered cigarette. Once a captain, now a private he knew his fate all too well. The corporal's mean 17-inch bayonet was pointed purposely at Private Ross Chambers. Chambers adjusted his rimless glasses.

Across the gap, the Jager sniper saw a flicker of light appear for a moment, gaining the moustached man's attention. His adjusted the focus with the meter dial. The periphery of the Otto Bock had a fisheye blur, but that did not matter. He had trained himself to overcome such obstacles. The glint from the cigarette was sufficient. The pressure on the trigger released the 8mm bullet which now crossed the gap as a blur. A second sound followed the first in symphony. The Jager man with the moustache slumped, the headshot fatal, death swift.

The corporal peered at the slumped body of the man dressed in khaki who had fallen in the British trench. The lens over his left eye was shattered and the socket now a black hole. The helmet had rolled over as the chin strap had sheared in the fall. He picked up the helmet and noticed how much lighter it was than his own Brodie. No-one called it a Brodie though. The corporal thought of it as his battle bowler, weighing just over 2lbs compared to this copy at ¾ lb. He brought his hobnailed boot down and the whole dome caved in easily. Two privates were summoned to remove the body of Private Ross Chambers.

Colonel Fleming surveyed the execution scene with some embarrassment. He walked back to his HQ and nodded to Robert Burnett.

'I think perhaps I was a fool and certainly misled Major Burnett. I hope your new rank will come through soon.'

Burnett recognised the humility that Fleming accepted.

'Colonel, I have learned through years of experience that many things are not quite as they appear. Of course General Hart's tragedy had to be dealt with, but Chambers was in fact a German spy and well placed to tell the enemy our plans. We look for little things and store these. When the Quartermaster noticed Chambers sifting through helmets after Lieutenant Hart's untimely death, he passed the message on. Some helmets had no stamp of origin like Dixon and Frith. Stan Bassett was a pawn in the whole story and he had been briefed by Chambers who had studied at Cambridge. His real name was Rudolph Kammer.'

'Clearly all of this is outside my league, Major, as I was fooled by this Kammer. But I must confess I would not have used Sergeant Miller as he's a troublemaker.'

'Ah, Colonel, this is where you have to be a little bit more world wise. Miller is an excellent marksman. The Germans have been picking off men right, left and centre up until now. It's an attrition of army's emotional capability. We could not allow any one German sniper to keep up their success, nor could we afford to see a man like Miller slowly die from the ravages of fever in Gallipoli. We now have one dead sniper and one dead spy. You will see more of Miller on the Western Front I think. It's all very convenient and wraps this contract up rather nicely don't you think?' And so two Germans rather than one were buried that morning on the Western Front.

Author's Note

As a child, I fitted an air raid warden's helmet (ARP) on my head while standing in a friend's garden shed. It was WW2 style and I staggered under the weight on my 13-year-old head. Designed to reduce some of the deadly effects of shrapnel and overhead explosives, the Brodie went into full manufacture in 1916. Firth and Sons, as with many steel manufacturers, helped develop the Type A which was later modified with manganese metal by Robert Hadfield. Whether anyone tried to con the British army I don't know, as my story is pure fiction. I certainly doubt Firth and Sons were involved in any such espionage and subterfuge as depicted by Stan Bassett in their factory at the Norfolk Works in Sheffield.

I should point out that David Lloyd-George was officially recognised as Minister for Munitions. Christopher Addison showed loyalty when supporting Lloyd-George in his bid for leadership of this party. Addison was made Minister thereafter. Later he was sacked in favour of a man who became rather more famous. Winston Leonard Spencer-Churchill became Minister for Munitions in June 1917.

Britain lagged behind the Germans in the skill of sniping, together with the optical equipment that made up the telescopic sight. On balance, the two rifles were equally capable and up to the job. Few snipers, as with young officers, mostly lieutenants, lasted long on the Western Front. Once Britain set up its sniper schools from 1915, the tide changed in the manner of the silent execution of soldiers and their officers. Our fictitious marksman, however, has a deeper backstory that begs to be told someday.

Perhaps of a lesser note and the British flag, its omission and status. Wales took on English law and was technically annexed under the British Crown in 1542. In

2021 the issue remains open to further debate in light of the Scottish National Party's bid for independence and Wales' rejection that it cannot be a principality but a country in its own right. Such matters however are beyond these pages.

OPERATION KALAVRYTA

CHICAGO, ILLINOIS, USA

The Hancock Centre should not be confused with the less than exciting cigarette box building similarly named in Boston, *Hancock Tower*. John Hancock was long dead, in fact he was a founding father, unlike Seymour Steinbeck, who was very much alive.

Steinbeck rubbed his thumb over the embossed gold label of his favourite tipple. The classic shaped bottle of Ron Zacapa contained 40% rum from the same-named village east of Guatemala. The connection? None really, except Steinbeck rented office space within the 856,000 square feet of the Hancock Center. Hancock used to import rum and had been antagonistic toward the British at the time of the Boston Tea Party. Unlike Hancock, who had spent time in Britain, Steinbeck was not entirely sure what the difference was between Britain, England and Scotland.

As he sipped his neat rum in a tapered brandy snifter, he savoured its honeyed butterscotch features, aided by the lone ice cube, as he looked out across Lake Michigan.

'Get me Bronson on the phone,' Steinbeck barked, expecting instant action. He was not a man who bathed words with pleasantries.

'Yes, Mr Steinbeck sir,' Ingrid his secretary responded.

He turned back to the computer to check his e-mails when the phone made a humming noise. He snatched at it.

'Bronson. Any news?'

The voice on the end of the phone eased his mood. Steinbeck's plump face cracked with more of a smirk than a smile. He sighed and sank into his soft padded leather chair. His gnarled nose sniffed the rum before enjoying another slug.

'So she's been found in London.' He paused and swallowed the dark nectar. 'Good, I want that bitch out of my life! Criton may have made a mistake, but she treated him as a self-styled killer.'

He replaced the phone on its cradle with uncanny gentleness. Seymour Steinbeck knew that Criton would not get out of prison for another five years, unless he were lucky. There was an inner fear that Criton would come to harm and so he arranged for him to have comfortable accommodation, and spread money around some bent prison guards to ensure his son's safety. He had already paid one officer and been deceived and vowed that would not happen again. A lesson was necessary so that no one would cross Seymour Steinbeck. Worse still, Criton's beauty would attract low life, and that would be worse. Criton had pulled a knife a few times, but always in self-defence. When he stabbed a kid from another school, the boy nearly died and had lost an arm as the limb could not be saved. He thought for a minute about the victim's name. It was weird, difficult to pronounce and not American. His mind failed for the moment so he turned to another person; a name well embroidered into his memory.

Officer Jennifer McAdam had told the court Criton came from a bad home and she had disciplined him on several occasions, saying he was unruly, drank and smoked. The idea that this described HIS little boy was preposterous. McAdam had made it up.

'My boy is good and goes to church on Sundays with the family,' Steinbeck had told Criton's prosecuting lawyer and judge. He had cursed himself when he realised he had not spent money on the best lawyer as had... that name again? He just could not recall the name of the father of his son's accuser.

Steinbeck felt Criton had been destined for good things and would have done well in school and later life had McAdam not interfered. The court had taken McAdam's side and the prosecutors had done the rest after the distraught victim had appealed to the jury's sensibilities, robbed of an arm.

Criton was a spoiled 17-year-old. Yes, his face was baby smooth and he looked more feminine than male, with no sign of anything other than light fluff under his nose. His lips were thin, his eyes mere slits and the face took on a cruel facade. He had hung around in a gang who clung to Criton because of his father's money. It was a classic case of spoiled brat, but Seymour loved him, as did Gunther, his aging father who lived with them.

McAdam was a policewoman who had worked at the 18th District police precinct on North Larrabee Avenue, so she knew the area well.

It was simple. As far as Steinbeck was concerned, McAdam took his son's prospects away, and now she would pay. Seymour L. Steinbeck had grown up in the slums of Chicago and had made his way standing up to the scum balls and shysters, never giving in. His father and mother had moved to the USA after the Second World War and it was hard making a new life. Gunther outlived his wife, adopted the American way of life but spoke English with a heavy German accent.

Seymour Steinbeck always paid his debts and kept his promises whichever side of the law was appropriate. Bronson dealt with diseased matters that affected his life, excising any cancers like a surgeon. His business lawyer, Henry Jacobsen, and Jim Bronson, his right hand man, kept his appearance squeaky clean. McAdam had tried to reach Steinbeck through Criton.

Bronson's loyalty was never in question. He knew where to look and his research found a freelance 'hit person'. The term seemed antiquated now. The contract was agreed upon and set in motion. There were no photos and all he cared about was a job done cleanly, with no lead back to him. Did he care who by and how? Hell no.

Steinbeck looked down at the family photograph on his polished redwood desk. Ingrid, his secretary, kept the neatly dusted frame pristine. March sunshine shone through the large windows of the tapered glass building, with its signature H football post masts at the top giving it a total height of 1500 feet. The address was 875 Michigan Avenue. The building was no longer the tallest in Chicago.

Steinbeck kept his jacket on, not because of the temperature, but for Prussian formality instilled into him by Gunther. The royal blue tie contrasted nicely with his cream shirt. Seymour's thinning sandy brown hair showed signs of balding. He reached for the photograph. In the picture Connie stood next to her husband. At her side their two daughters, Philly and Jessica, then

Seymour Junior and Criton. Criton was 14 years old in the picture taken three years earlier. He had made his father, born into good German stock, so proud. Sadness caught him and then a sense of anger arose. Bile crept into his throat. The Pepto-Bismol he kept in the drawer soon soothed the heartburn. He cursed the attack. Lack of exercise did little to help his overweight size. Dr Norman, his physician, had warned him about his blood pressure, and he took tablets each day to keep this under control.

Nonetheless, even tablets failed to subdue the stress entirely. Although not sentimental, Seymour wiped away a tear. His family was his life, his pride, and even when they made errors he was quick to forgive, but not so others.

'Yes, indeed McAdam will pay,' he told himself. 'Zanguthran' came highly recommended. Frustration gave way to his memory lapse and he picked the phone up. 'Bronson, what was the name of that kid that Criton injured?'

STANSTED AIRPORT, LONDON, UK

Jenny McAdam placed her paperback in her shoulder bag. 'Flight FR118' blinked, showing 'Gate 42' on the electronic screen. She needed to be one of the first 90 passengers to reach the gate lounge to take advantage of the overhead storage. Travelling on cheap flights was okay, but it was like wading through treacle; human bodies and trailing bags on wheels tangled in a sea of chaos.

Discipline soon disappeared when passengers were herded and given a choice. The scene was unfriendly, one she knew all too well from back in Chicago. That had been her problem; the hostility and mindless violence. These last few years had been more relaxed. She had forced herself to reach an inner calm, but it had not been easy. Escape had been her way out. She eyed the line which seemed to divide passengers into who had paid for 'Fast Track', and 'The Rest'. She was in the latter group. A pleasant enough woman lifted her microphone and repeated the command.

'Will all passengers waiting for Flight FR118 move to the left to allow priority passengers to pass.'

The assortment of multicoloured, multi-shaped luggage shifted like zombies, scraping along the floor, clogging up what little space existed. Squashed between two groups, Jenny now had to put up with two girls chatting incessantly. Despite the weather being a cool seven degrees Centigrade, a considerable amount of flesh was on parade. Variegated hair colours collaborated with nose piercings and tattoos circumnavigating the arm from shoulder to elbow of the taller of the two. The conversation was banal. The second girl held her maroon passport in her left hand. Jenny was surprised to see the embossed coat of arms in gold nearly scrubbed out.

'Wow, that's one overused passport!' she thought.

A nudge into the small of her back pushed her forward. She found the temptation for retaliation until the voice uttered an apology and saved her an embarrassing altercation. The line settled down.

She thought 'line' and chuckled inwardly. The Brits liked to use 'queue' instead of 'line'. How quaint!

The large windows facing the aircraft provided a glimpse of the gloomy day. Light rain glistened on the wet surface as the Boeing 737-800 appeared, the staple jet used by the budget airline.

'Christ, the goddam plane has only just arrived. How much longer are we to wait?' she thought. A woman spoke on her mobile to her right, the voice too far away to make out. People talking subtracted her ability to make out the accent. A man a few inches taller, with greying hair stood by the woman. Jenny assumed they were married. They looked cosy.

A couple, maybe in their early twenties, were clinging to each other as if separation meant they would float away into space. Jenny smiled at the thought of the first spring of love in a relationship. Slurping kisses punctuated the moment. A baby started crying, so her mother picked her up to soothe her. A young father leant in to pat down the little head devoid of hair. With some jostling the crying ceased and the regulatory bottle with dummy happily slid into the baby's mouth. Two airline staff walked past, avoiding the crush. Bright red hats and uniforms covered by raincoats offered an image of order. The flight officer and female staff member nodded to check-in staff inspecting passports and vouchers and trying to activate the scanner over mobile phones for those wise enough to use the smartphone app.

Jenny could see staff climbing off the plane. One white-haired man, presumably the pilot, was talking to two armed officers carrying submachine guns. Her trained eye recognised the compact folding Heckler and Koch semi-automatics favoured by the police in the UK. The gun's 9mm bullets could reach over 600 feet at a rate of 800 per minute.

'Christ, I'm sad to know these sorta facts.'

Her eyes swung wide to where a tall man stood dressed in a dark blue suit. His physique suggested he looked after himself. Clean shaven, square jaw and thickish neck suggested military. His neat light brown coloured hair looked natural and cropped at the sides. Her eyes traced his waistline. The belt line was not disturbed by a paunch as it was with the man she had spotted earlier standing next to the woman with the mobile. No, he looked military. His shoes were black and shone with that detail and care instilled into those in uniform. Perhaps she stared too long, for he looked directly at her and nodded.

'That's plain creepy,' she thought. Not that she minded if he looked at her; she was good-looking, she knew and in good shape herself. It was the confidence of his gaze. The command was instantly recognisable by how they held their posture. Facial reactions could show fear, shock, comedy. This guy showed none of these patterns; he was gazing with intent and it was not sexual. She turned away, slightly frightened. The rise and fall of her neat bosom was rapid until she realised she was almost hyperventilating.

'No, it can't be, surely, I am too far away from home.'

THE PLANE

'Do you want the window seat?' Flynn asked.

'Thanks, think I'll snooze,' Jane replied looking at his clean shaven face.

'Shit, these seats are tight, you can hardly breathe if you bend down,' he grumbled.

Flynn grunted as he reached for the bag tucked under his feet. His large stomach stopped him as the air from his lungs was squeezed uncomfortably.

'Suppose the mobile phone needs setting to flight mode? Stupid really, planes don't fall out of the air. Anyway, phone masts aren't that high.'

Jane ignored his comments. Flynn was 55, his wife a few years younger. She looked in good shape, her shoulder length hair had flecks of grey.

Looking at the notice stuck to the back of the seat he announced, 'One hundred and eighty-nine passengers and the seats don't recline. There are no tables and this storage is hopeless. It all has to go under the seat or into the locker above.'

'Stop complaining. You wanted a cheap flight and that's what you've got, now chill out!' Jane said and went back to her attempts to sleep.

Flynn clicked his seatbelt closed before being asked and tried to settle. Passengers bobbed up and down, fitting their cases above their seats or wherever a space arose. There was always one passenger who sneaked through far more luggage than entitled, despite all the repetitive checks. It was difficult to walk very far once entering departures before having to show the flimsy computer printed voucher and passport.

Kyle Ritter, the tall man in the dark blue suit, stood two rows behind Jenny. She kept snatching furtive glances. Since passing from the crowded lounge to the steps of the plane, her fear, if not phobia, had grown. Ritter made no effort to contact her. She heard him say little, but had noted his American accent during his entry onto the plane. When the steward asked him if he was well today, he just said,

'Sure thing, thanks.'

The olive-skinned stewardess had noticed Kyle and admired his strong features and physique. Jenny had missed little; maybe it was her training?

'Christ, am I going mad?' she thought.

'Please take your seats as soon as you can to allow passengers through,' an accented male voice spoke over the aircraft communications system. The instructions might have been reasonable had this been an ocean liner, but the cramped space left little room to move. Some lockers were too high so that passengers needed assistance. Everyone was doing their best.

Jenny carried a small rucksack as well as her shoulder bag. Two retractable walking poles stuck out. Somewhat frustrated at being moved, she saw Jane and Flynn and recognised them from the gate lounge. Flynn had his head turned to Jane and so did not see Jenny as she struggled to turn. Two retractable poles projected a good 18 inches from the rucksack and made an arc, connecting with Flynn.

'Whoa there,' he uttered, fearful of being poked in the eye or risking damage to his expensive glasses. 'Come in and have a seat won't you?'

'Gee, sorry, it's a tight squeeze. I brought this for my mother as she is disabled and needs some walking sticks.'

Flynn thought this improbable. The blue sticks seemed thin and flimsy for any disabled person, unless of course she was a lightweight?

He smiled. 'Tight fit these planes!'

Jenny slid the backpack off her shoulder and the weight indented the leather seat as it fell. She tucked the poles further in and hoisted the pack up until she could slide the luggage into the overhead cubby hole, leaving the curved flap up for the aeroplane staff to close.

'Wow, good to make it. I had to change seats.'

Flynn noticed her Midwest accent; the edges seemed softened so he thought, maybe Canadian. The different styles and tones of North American timbres were always tricky, yet this woman clearly lived in the UK. Back home she would reassert those vowels and consonants, no doubt. He took in her trim body and height. Straight, neat blonde hair just touched her shoulders. A sharp nose gave strength to her face. She sat down.

'Jenny,' she said, offering her hand.

She liked Flynn. Maybe it was the kind face; he seemed patient, possibly attentive, unlike many men she knew. The altercation with the poles had not fazed him.

Flynn shook her hand exchanging their names warmly at the same time. The woman's skin appeared cold but firm in grip; unusual for a female, he thought.

'Going to Athens?' It was a stupid question really, he started to think. Where else was the Athens flight going, unless of course she was flying on somewhere, which was entirely possible?

'Yes,' she answered.

Tell-tale lines around her eyes put her age at late forties. Flynn saw she used moderate foundation on her face, but it was not pretentiously thick. Her jeans fitted well, showing off her rounded hips, and the flat stomach suggested she kept fit.

As Jenny sat she brushed her neat blue jeans, then placed a light brown leather bag under the seat as commanded by the airplane staff. The voice of the cabin officer kept cutting in. The interruptions annoyed her.

Flynn turned back to Jane. With her eyes closed, she seemed to dismiss the conversation. Flynn decided to ask Jenny some light-hearted questions about the recent appointment of the new president.

'So are you in UK to avoid Uncle Donald?'

The American smiled. 'No, of course not.' Her forehead wrinkled and she stretched her mouth into a leer. 'The man is acting like Hitler, if not trying to take on his mantle. Just like Hitler's inner circle, he has established men loyal to him, and not just that, they wear special badges, just like Hitler's men did. That's freaky don't you think?'

There was a certain amount of hysteria to her voice. Flynn changed tack.

'So you like the UK then? Have you been to Oxford, for example?'

'I've never been to Oxford but I just love Cambridge. I don't know a lot about Oxford.'

Flynn mentioned a detective called Morse – a character that had screened on British TV for several decades. No, she had never heard of Morse, so Oxford was a dead subject.

'So where do you come from, I mean originally?'

North Carolina, it's real nice,' she ventured. 'I like the beaches there. They're quieter than further south.'

Flynn recalled Carolina was in the south and part of the confederacy. 'You know we supported the south in the American Civil War. We bombarded the Union fleet in Charleston.'

'So you're a professor?'

'No, I'm not that clever!' Flynn replied. 'I work in IT. So what do you do, Jenny?'

She used her hand to brush her hair as if it was out of place. Even though her hair was fine, she just needed to assure herself, not that Flynn caught such subtleties.

'Er, I'm responsible for caring for women who have been assaulted. I was working in Germany but prefer the UK. It has similar standards to the US and you just feel kinda more comfortable.'

'And what did you do in the States?'

'Locked people up!'

There was a pause as she looked toward the aisle. 'I was a police officer,' her tone softening so as not to be overheard.

'Guess you had to make some difficult decisions,' avoiding the usual dumb question – '*Did you kill anyone yet?*'

'Sure, we had to deal with some real low life.' Flynn was easy to talk to and kinda cute. 'I loved my job but there is always a cost to the whole cop thing,' she said, not wanting to appear too engaging, and then again not dismissive.

Flynn liked talking to cops but rarely had the chance to speak to a real live ex-policewoman.

'So what do you think about people carrying guns?'

'I think they should be allowed – open in holsters like Texas and Alaska where you can see them – only two states do this,' she said.

'Why those states?'

'In Alaska they carry them for protection from animals! Yes, from age six up they can do this. They're trained to defend themselves, you know with bear guns. It's justified.'

'Surely the urban man does not need such weaponry, especially if the guns are concealed?'

'All police officers have to take the view that people are carrying. We had a case recently where the cops had to go to a pawn store and borrow some automatic guns so they could take on a gang with better weapons.'

'doesn't taking a bigger gun to a battle just entice the bad guys to take better weaponry, Flynn said.

'Obama tried to stop it but was unsuccessful. You know our gun lobby is pretty powerful,' she said

'We don't carry guns in the UK, do you feel unsafe?' Flynn said.

'Yes, sure I do but not in the same way. I'm constantly worried about people I've locked up and what they might do. I'm always on the alert.'

They talked films, Flynn had to mention *Lock, Stock and Two Smoking Barrels*, a Brit film with guns.

'Sorry, I've got to get up,' finding she needed to use the bathroom.

Flynn kindly hit the alert light. He pointed, 'The seatbelt sign says stay, better let them know.'

Jenny returned and the plane started to descend. Thick Greek-accented English cut in, giving instructions. Her lips were bright orange, the makeup made her feel more confident as a woman.

VENIZELOS AIRPORT, GREECE

Jenny held up her blue US passport and went through police check without difficulties. Ritter stood directly behind her and seemed to have a problem. Flynn and Jane held their maroon European passports up and likewise passed through. Some form of commotion had erupted, with Ritter appearing angry and distressed. Jenny smiled. Her tip-off had worked. Ritter would be dragged off to a room and searched, and they would find the evidence she suspected. No doubt he was a hit man. He had all the right MO. She felt proud that she had acted to neutralise the risk and recalled how attentive the senior member of cabin staff had been when pointed out that she was an ex-police officer in the USA.

'Yes, Officer, with all the terrorism around we take these matters seriously. We'll radio ahead and have someone take off this man. Don't worry, we can handle it from here.'

Jenny turned to see Jane and Flynn talking together and could overhear their conversation.

'How about we grab a coffee first? I need a hit and the stuff on the plane was crap.'

The passengers from Flight FR118 had deplaned and were now flooding into the corridors. Some headed for the toilets while others looked for their luggage on the snaking carousels.

'All right, but let's get the luggage first, then you can gorge on caffeine if you must.'

Jane's voice had risen as the noise of Ritter being dragged away by two burly policemen with sidearms caught everyone's attention. Flynn and Jane ignored the commotion and started to follow Jenny.

The light green case had wheels. Jenny extended the handle after checking the tag and started pulling the bag toward the entrance. Flynn was not far behind. Jenny turned and smiled to say goodbye...

Flynn lurched forward but was intercepted by two children who cut across him, separating Jenny who entered the door marked '*Toualetes ton gynaikon*'.

Two women were in the facility, one at the sink and one exiting the cubicle.

'Oh, hello, I'd not realised it was you.'

Jane looked at Jenny. 'Airports are busy places,' she said.

'If you are thinking of going into the toilet cubicle with your case and backpack, it's going to be a bit tight.'

'Yeah, I need to go as it is a bit of a drive to the villa.'

'Let me look after the bags while you go in. I'm in no hurry.'

'Thanks, that's nice of you.'

The area was now free for the time being. Jenny entered the cubicle.

Jenny sat on the toilet, slumped against the toilet partition, her mouth hanging open. A dribble of dark blood ran down her cheek. One of the sharp ends of the retractable walking pole was embedded in the side of her neck, otherwise there was little to show for the violence. The toilet door was locked so that several hours had passed since Jane had met Jenny. The cleaner had radioed for help but Jenny was dead at the scene. Ritter, having disentangled himself from the police, left the airport.

Jane left Flynn at the airport entrance while she took a pre-arranged taxi. 'Thanks Jeff, she said to the man she had called Flynn, 'see you stateside in a few days. You did a great job. You make one irritating husband!'

A car pulled up as Jeff climbed into his taxi.

'Everything all right?' the driver asked.

'Sure, why wouldn't it be?'

'Where to then?'

'72 Poseidonos Avenue,' Jane replied.

Her cell phone rang. A voice spoke. 'Zanguthran?'

'Z here.'

'What status do we have now?'

'Permanent retirement!'

'The money will be wired to the usual account.'

The woman called Z and previously called Jane switched the phone off; no pleasantries, this was business. Zanguthran was her code name and she was not English or American but Israeli.

CHICAGO – STEINBECK'S HOME

'Well?' Bronson put the phone back in his pocket. 'All done, Mr Steinbeck.'

'Good, sort out the details.' His cigar ash splashed over the ashtray.

'Oh, honey, you're making a mess with these darn smokes. You really oughta quit,' Connie chided.

'Not tonight, Connie, we're going out to celebrate and taking Father out as well, he'll like that.'

The phone rang again. Bronson picked it up. The look on his mellow face altered.

'What is it Bronson, who is it?'

Bronson's face seemed to have lost its colour. The next few hours would not be pleasant…

VENIZELOS AIRPORT, GREECE

Z, alias Jane, alias someone unknown, pulled her hairpiece off, revealing short, dark hair. Suddenly she was not so old.

'So, did the police go easy on you?' Turning to the driver.

'Piece of cake, Z. Case of mistaken identity. I'm just an associate professor at Sonoma State University,' Ritter replied.

The smartphone vibrated. Zanguthran looked down and deftly tapped in the access code.

> MESSAGE:
> ACCIDENT ST CHARLES CORRECTIONAL
> CENTRE. YOUTH CRITON STEINBECK 17
> DEAD. CAUSE SUICIDE.

She produced a cigarette from her bag and lit the end. Throwing her head back she exhaled the smoke.

'Thought you'd given up?'

'I have, but one now and then…'

'Good news?'

'Put it this way,' she paused for effect, 'Governor Bruce Rauner now has some more pressure on him, and the Illinois Department of Juvenile Justice is going to have to do some explaining.'

'So, two contracts in one?' Ritter asked.

'Not quite, Ritter, just one left, this is a Triple Contract. Now you are driving me to see Mr

Mandrapilios.' The car pulled up at the address. 'You stay here and wait while I sort the final part out.'

CHICAGO – STEINBECK'S HOME

Evander Mandrapilios had been the name Steinbeck could not remember, although Jim Bronson reminded him over the phone that Criton had maimed Angelino Mandrapilios in the knife fight. Mandrapilios was not unlike Steinbeck. Both held grudges. His mantra had been, 'hit back twice as hard'.

He had grown up during the Nazi occupation of Greece and so had a different view on life. Nazis had killed his family in a callous execution.

'Ah Zanguthran, good of you to come. What news?' Mandrapilios said.

Z rarely saw her employers face to face but Evander Mandrapilios had known her as a young girl and she had done work for him before.

'Criton hanged himself. He must have felt real remorse at hurting Angelino.' There was little humour in her voice.

'Any loose ends?'

'No we had an inmate lean on someone who made it look like an accident. All dues will be paid as usual.'

Z's network was extensive. 'And the last part of the contract?'

'Jeff's flying back and we will return to Chicago later today on separate planes.'

'I'd offer you a drink but I know you don't imbibe and doubtless have to return, but thanks for coming out of your way.'

Evander Mandrapilios kissed Z on her cheek. 'Your father would be proud of you,' his Greek accent breaking through his otherwise fluent English.

'The woman you despatched?'

'Steinbeck wanted her removed as she had double crossed him and testified as you knew she would. McAdam's real crime was her involvement running a prostitution ring in Germany with girls from Turkey and Bosnia. Some of these profits went back to Steinbeck's organisation. She was siphoning money off the profit due to Steinbeck. The BfV reached out, not wanting to be involved, and provided evidence that two Israeli girls had become caught up in this web of criminal activity.' Z pronounced the BfV as in German, *Bundesamt für Verfassungsschutz*, her German accent near perfect.

'McAdam knew the local police were investigating her in Cologne. She skipped across into Britain using a false passport to start up again. Mossad called us to take care of the problem as part of a cross-border relationship. The Federal Office for the Protection of the Constitution, better known as the BfV, wanted an arm's length approach.'

'I trust you will take care of the last part of the contract for me. I have wired the money to your Swiss bank account.' Evander trusted the woman named Zanguthran implicitly, as though she was his daughter.

CHICAGO, HANCOCK BUILDING

Connie and Seymour Steinbeck were inconsolable for some time after learning about Criton's suicide. Gunther cried uncontrollably; he loved his wayward grandson and saw something of himself in the boy. Steinbeck was unconvinced that Criton had hanged himself. He had ordered Bronson to reach out for contacts. Leaving his office he headed for elevator 2 with Bronson selecting the car park on the tenth floor. Bronson pushed the button. A hundred floors made up the Hancock Centre and the Otis lift could travel at 1800 feet per second, or around 20mph. The elevator descended but then stopped abruptly so that the two men fell against the wall. The elevator started again as the men straightened, but seemed to make a strange noise. The indicator system appeared to show the floors passing very quickly. The lift had lost some of the system's braking and was now gaining speed rapidly, reaching terminal velocity and hurtling at over 50 mph. Steinbeck noticed the weightlessness first and then almost a sense of elation. His stomach felt strange as his internal organs moved under the enormous gravitational shift in forces. Memories of the past days came back and then nothing...

Jeff looked very different from the man who had sat next to Jane on Flight FR118 as he drove down the circular exit road from the centre. He wondered how well the ceiling heaters worked as they lined the overhang intended to keep ice down. His job had been to ensure that no one entered the elevator when Steinbeck left his office. Under the annual inspection programme, independent inspectors serviced some 22,000 elevators so the task of sabotaging the braking system had not been that hard, given his background in engineering. He could fashion a tool from any piece of metal or blow the wheel off a car cleanly. The fire brigade would be on their way but no one could help Mr Steinbeck and his assistant Mr Bronson.

Evander Mandrapilios picked up his phone in Athens. 'Have you seen the news? Another elevator failure at Michigan Avenue. Unfortunately a Mr Steinbeck and one of his employees has died tragically.' Z ended the call. Evander Mandrapilios looked down at his file.

The report was marked **'SECRET'**:

> SS UNTERSTURMFURHER (SEKOND LEUTNANT)
> GUNTHER STEINBECK WAS GIVEN HARD LABOUR
> FOR HIS PART IN OPERATION KALAVRYTA ON 10
> DECEMBER 1943 WHEN ORDERED BY GENERAL
> VON LE SUIRE OF 117TH JÄGER DIVISION TO
> MURDER GREEK CIVILIANS. THE GERMANS
> REACHED KALAVRYTA ON DECEMBER 9. IN THE
> EARLY MORNING OF DECEMBER 13, 1943, THE
> GERMANS ROUNDED UP ALL TOWN RESIDENTS AND
> FORCED THEM INTO THE SCHOOL BUILDING WHERE
> THEY SEPARATED THE OLDER BOYS AND MEN FROM
> THE WOMEN AND CHILDREN. AFTER LOOTING THE
> TOWN AND SETTING IT ABLAZE, THE GERMANS
> MACHINE-GUNNED THE MEN. FOUR HUNDRED
> THIRTY-EIGHT MEN AND OLDER BOYS WERE
> KILLED.
>
> CURRENT WHEREABOUTS: EMIGRATED USA
> 1946. DOMICILED – CHICAGO, USA. FAMILY SON
> SEYMOUR STEINBECK AND FAMILY.

He studied the old black and white family picture resting on his thick, polished wooden cedar desk showing a young Evander with his two brothers, sister, mother and father, who all perished that day in Kalavryta—dated 1943. Evander was the only one who escaped.

Author's note

The triple contract weaves through three actions taken by the multilingual female assassin Zanguthran and her two colleagues linked to Israel and a Greek named Evander. During our first year of marriage I took my wife to Chicago and we enjoyed a cocktail on the 95th observation floor of the tapered design of the Hancock Centre. In 2018 the centre changed its name to 875 Michigan Avenue. Like many tall buildings, it stood out and made a valuable backdrop for Seymour Steinbeck's story.

However, my main story started on a flight with EasyJet to Athens from London Stansted in 2017 again with my wife. A female ex-police officer from the USA nearly poked my eyes out with her walking poles. She intended to meet her mother. I portrayed myself as the man with a large stomach and talked to her when she told me the story of how she had to leave the USA after putting a young boy in prison. The conversation was a synopsis of the actual dialogue that took place. Of course the fictional characters were actors playing to put McAdam at ease.

My wife slept through most of the flight but seeing me chatting up this rather attractive woman; words were said later on as you can imagine! Nonetheless, Jenny McAdam became the blueprint for the story. Whatever her real name was, Jenny did help re-house girls in Germany before moving to Cambridge in the UK, so this was all true.

The twist in the tale came from an actual event in 1943 called Operation Kalavryta when Nazi troops exacted terrible massacres on innocent people during the Greek guerrilla war. Second Lieutenant Gunther Steinbeck was part of fiction, but General von le Suire was not.

A STRANGE AFFAIR

Simon and Alison Rayden left England on a rainy day for their two-week honeymoon and flew first class into Hong Kong's Chek Lap Kok airport. Alison had a deep secret and felt insecure about telling her new husband the truth. The marriage contract requires honesty up front and she had failed.

The newlyweds took the shuttle to Harbour Plaza North Point Hotel. Downtown Hong Kong appeared jam-packed with traffic and high-rise buildings. Few buildings were less than ten stories high. Hong Kong was a business centre and shouted out with flashing neon signs, radiating messages far and wide, as boats sailed between the islands.

'This place doesn't have much room, does it, Simon.'

'No, and the domestic accommodation is so highly prized it produces costly real estate,' he replied. Buses, taxis and trams were all vying for business.

At the hotel, jetlag kept them awake so they made love until the early hours, when sleep finally came with spent exhaustion.

The following day, when all others had finished their food and gone off sightseeing, the honeymooners ate a hearty breakfast, having slept longer due to jet lag. Later, they found the nearest underground railway or MTR, with its curious sign, two U's top-to-tail. Street markets appeared with fresh fruit and the eager bustle as people sought food at midday. Alison looked at the ducks which hung loosely from hooks in rows decorating the frontages.

'That's put me off eating Peking duck from now on. Don't they look scrawny?'

Simon added, 'I am more worried about the hygiene!'

The sounds of downtown Hong Kong attacked their ears. Traffic lights sounded more like a hammering out musical crotchets. As the lights changed to green, the beats intensified. Simon explained that the rhythm adjusted to aid the blind.

Investigating the downtown alleys and open supermarkets seemed an excellent way to spend their first day. Alison insisted on buying a blue silk Chinese dress. 'What do you think of this then?' she asked Simon.

Simon was not a big one for shopping when you did not necessarily need an item, and he was even worse at choosing for women, so he was suddenly out of his comfort zone. He improvised.

'I think that is a great colour and would look fabulous on you,' satisfied that Alison would be happy with this supportive remark.

'Perhaps the red one is better?' she quizzed him again.

'Yes, the red one is perhaps better,' he said, trying to please her.

'So you don't like the blue as much as the red?' She seemed irritated with the way the dialogue was going.

'Er, no, the blue is nice as well, I just agreed with you.'

'But I need an honest opinion, Simon!'

'Well if you cannot choose and you like both of them, have them both!' he suggested.

She smiled instantly. 'I like that idea,' knowing she had manoeuvred him into an impossible position. Her feminine guile won out. 'Come on, I'll buy you a coffee,' as they walked away from the shop.

Simon knew a trump card when he saw one, but he grabbed her waist and squeezed, simultaneously kissing her on the lips. As they passed an alley, Simon saw a small quaint shop that attracted his attention. He peered in through a window made of a single piece of glass. It offered a good view of the mystical atmosphere inside. Shelving contained glass jars and stoppers of different sizes. The arrangement of small animal skulls appeared in strategic locations. The massive amethyst rock stood out in the centre of a round wooden table with large candles placed around the outside. The purple colouring had different shades. As he surveyed the array of contents, he spotted a green and orange patterned hexagonal object with a mirror in the centre.

'Hey, Alison hold on there, come and look at this. I have always been interested in the occult. Can we go in? That's a Ba Gua Mirror used in traditional Asian Witchcraft. It's a bit like Tarot cards. It has eight sides and trigrams that divide into different spiritual locations.'

'Isn't it a bit creepy, Simon? Anyway, how do you know all of this stuff?'

'No, it's harmless stuff unless you believe it.'

As they entered the little shop, the smell of incense hit them. It was powerful and had a sweet odour, but with a floral infusion. A giant Buddha statue stood in one corner with the right hand and palm-held at shoulder level. Simon realised there were no electric lights, only candles and the natural light coming from the large window illuminating the shop.

'Gur mawring sir, come in and pleeze look awound. We haf much for you to see here,' a young Chinese woman in her thirties spoke enthusiastically. Although she could speak English, she had the usual difficulties with letters strange to Eastern tongues. They could understand her easily enough.

Alison and Simon browsed a while, picking objects up, comparing finds. 'Ha, look at this,' as she lifted one of the tiny skulls. 'This would be something that wouldn't worry you but I hate to think what the story is for it to be so small.'

'Maybe the Tarot cards are more "you"?' he suggested.

'I don't believe in all that future prediction stuff,' she said.

The Chinese woman, overhearing her, interjected.

'Naw it is true you can learnalotta thing from card, lady. Come this way I show you.'

Simon saw reluctance written on her face as she passed toward the back of the shop. Coloured strands guarded an otherwise open entrance. He made a face and threw his hands up. She looked back as if to say, 'I don't want to go', but she did. The strips with their coloured beads clacked as Alison passed through and collided with her face and shoulders. The last two strips of beads slipped off her shoulder, falling back to their previous position in the doorway.

A little woman of indefinable age sat behind a thick oak desk. Her name was Ying Ma, her first name meaning Clever Eagle. The fortune-teller scene could have been from anywhere in the world. She looked at Alison seriously and beckoned for her to sit down. Twenty-two Tarot cards based on the Greater Secrets or Major Arcana lay on the table. Ying Ma turned several cards face down while discarding others. There were no suits in this card selection. She selected six randomly and arranged them in a row. Ying Ma used the Tarot cards for Europeans to give a mystical aura. She was well versed in other methods of fortune and even used the *I Ching,* taken from the ancient Chinese *Book of Changes*. The system entailed various broken and unbroken patterns called hexagrams. Europeans only needed simple methods, although the Tarot card was initially Italian, not Chinese!

Alison sat down and the younger woman stood behind her.

'She now makes you fortune and I tell you wat she say.' The young girl was well practised in building an illusion associated with the occult.

Alison decided to sit back. The older woman's face looked like leather, with deep flaccid creases. Her teeth were poor, her nose small and stubby and her hair thin and grey. Alison thought she must be a hundred and fifty! Close by a candle burned with two joss sticks supported in tall thin glass holders. The scent was strong, if not overpowering. It seemed different to the joss sticks she had used when visiting friends as a teenager. They had been all the rage then.

Ying Ma turned the cards over. The candle flickered. There was no wind but the candle seemed to shift of its own accord. The light altered so darkness transcended the room. Alison thought this was all an act.

The older woman reacted and spoke rapidly.

'What's she saying?' Alison asked the younger.

'I dunno, she upset about somfin!'

The old soothsayer rocked back and forwards then leaned forward and grabbed Alison's hand. The cards lying on the table had previously depicted individual scenes of The Magician, The High Priestess, The Empress, The Lovers, Wheel of Fortune, Justice and The Hangman, but now skeletal Death, riding a horse with a scythe in his left hand, replaced each. On the top of the card known as Death, 'numeral XIII' appeared within a scroll.

'What does this mean?' not liking the image very much.

Alison felt a shiver go up to her spine, despite the confined space and the heat of the day. The younger women spoke to the older, and after receiving a brief despatch of words, she simply turned to Alison. 'You go now berrer kwick. Bad omen lady, prease go kwick!'

Simon saw Alison exit the small room, looking the colour of alabaster. 'Hey there, what happened to you?' he asked.

'Come, we need to leave,' Alison said urgently.

'But why?' he asked.

'I'll tell you. NOW COME,' The squeal her voice made caused him alarm.

They found somewhere on the corner to have drinks.

'No I don't want coffee. Give me something stronger!' They ordered and she knocked back her wine quickly.

'So come on, Alison, what happened? You look worried, darling.'

'I am not sure, the experience was strange. I'm sure it was all put on, but I have seen card tricks before. You should have seen her, Simon, she was over a hundred I reckon, and all wrinkled.' She went on. 'As I stared at the cards, the light went dark for a moment and I thought that the candle was going to go out. The cards remained visible the whole time and I saw each one fade and then change to the face of Death. You know that awful picture of Death carrying his scythe?'

'Yeah, right, that doesn't mean anything. Death doesn't always depict doom, as you know.'

The expression on Alison's face suggested that she was not convinced.

What she had not known or could not see was that a long shadow had entered that small room causing the candle to gut. The old woman had felt the aura, despite being unable to see him. Bright light accompanied a dark apparition momentarily. Without the sightseeing powers of the mystic, Alison had seen and felt nothing.

Life on the streets of Hong Kong had been hard for the older woman called Ying Ma, aged 92 and well respected. She had made many predictions until a leader from a Chinese gang known as the Triads had threatened her after she'd predicted the death of his first born. The child, a girl, died and so the old leader was not so bothered, on account of girls having less value than boys, but her presence was feared. Better she practised on foreigners while hidden away in her shop. Foreigners were easy targets and no one minded when *Laowai* were ripped off.

Today, all things had changed. Ying Ma and Alison stared at the cards. The face of the cards altered in front of her. Death would visit Alison with complete certainty, not once but twice.

As Ying Ma sat following Alison's departure, the anxiety caused by the atmosphere around her was infectious. The temperature of the stuffy room started to descend. Ying Ma had only seen this occur once before, and she knew her fate.

Later that afternoon the younger woman, Xiaoling Deng, brought her aunt some tea and found her slumped back in her chair. She moved her aunt's arm to wake her, but she was dead. The lines on her face were smooth in death.

Alison's secret was now causing tightness in her chest. She had to tell Simon, but that could end their love, marriage and all that had come true. The couple returned to the hotel exhausted from so much walking, and the jetlag, which still presented an effort. The air was warm still at 8 pm. The events of the day had dissipated as they headed for bed early, falling into each other's arms. Alison put on her carefully chosen nightie, only to have it taken off again immediately. Sometimes their lovemaking was slow and gentle; other times lust and hunger for each other took over. They soon knew more about themselves, having explored each other spiritually and physically. Alison traced some of Simon's creases sensitively with her finger. 'You saying I am ageing?' Simon admonished.

'Of course you are, but that shows your maturity. A face forms a rich tapestry, mapping life's ups and downs. None of us is perfect and this makes us unique. I would hate to look the same as everyone else.'

'Alison Rayden, perhaps you should have been a poet, but you better not be saying I am as creased as that little old woman you talked about?'

They planned each day over breakfast, poring over the tourist book that Simon had bought in the bookstore in Manchester. He wanted to take Alison to the top of the mountain overlooking downtown Hong Kong and Victoria Harbour. They reached Kennedy Road and worked out how to stop the tram mid-climb to the peak after paying HK $72. The peak funicular railway was steep and the view was breath-taking when the mist cleared. As the train ascended, Alison clung to Simon and he pressed himself to her, hand pushed into the back pocket of her jeans. Alison, unabashed, pressed against him, staring into his eyes with a smile from ear to ear.

The peak had an enormous multi-storeyed glass building with numerous escalators. Alison took some snaps of the scenery, and plenty of Simon.

'Let's get a picture of us,' she suggested.

The usual selfie created laughter as parts of the body were cut off until they had it just about right, even though their eyes seemed enormous because of the angle of the photo. They took seats at a bar called Bubba Gump's and ordered daiquiri cocktails. After a light bite, they caught the funicular back down, re-joining the heaving mass below.

Alison looked over her cocktail glass. 'You know, Simon, I still cannot get my head around that fortune teller. It all seemed so real. I suppose it is the look on that old woman's face that keeps coming back to haunt me.' She went back to noisily sucking the icy contents through a straw.

'Put it out of your head. The whole thing was clearly an illusion, set up to mislead you. Think of it as high-class entertainment. There is no such thing as fortune-telling, it works based on common association. A bit like the stars, you know, the Zodiac signs that you see in papers. There is usually one common sentence that fits all cases. I view it as hocus-pocus. Now come on, we should focus on all the things the city has to offer.'

'I am sure you are right. The light did fade and I guess that was where the card switch came in. Maybe it was just an elaborate card trick. I mean I only paid 15 Hong Kong dollars.'

That was the last time Alison and Simon talked about Ying Ma or her niece, Xiaoling Deng, not that they knew or could pronounce the names. They were two Chinese people lost in a city with a massive population. Plucking up courage, Alison took Simon to a Japanese restaurant and decided she had to come clean.

First she ordered chicken teriyaki, a sashimi selection and dark miso soup, as Simon had not experienced this cuisine. She showed him how to use the chopsticks, dipping sashimi into the dark teriyaki sauce and then special horseradish. Pressing the delicate fish into his mouth, he acknowledged the succulence, and then his eyes popped out as the dose of green horseradish caused him to erupt with the heat. His eyes started to water and so looked to quench the fire in his mouth using his Tsing Tao beer. 'Christ, are you trying to kill me, you little devil?' he chastised her.

She dipped her finger into some drinking water then pushed it into his mouth to soothe his tongue, while he sucked on the appendage lasciviously.

She looked at him with an expression that stopped him in his tracks.

'What? I know that expression.'

'Simon, there's something I've got to tell you. I've not been sincere.'

Alison had not wanted to use the word honest as it wasn't dishonesty as such, but she knew that she could have been more open. But then the question would have arisen was she mad?

'Should I be worried?' he asked.

'I've been married before.'

'Yes, I know, and the fact that he had died. So, is that your secret?'

'No. The man I married was you.'

'What? We only met eighteen months ago and you were married...'

'...yes for ten years. Look.'

Alison showed Simon a picture of a man who looked identical to him.

'Doppelganger!'

'No, it's not. When you first came into my office that day, I was shocked. You didn't see the desk photo because I made sure I removed it.'

Simon leaned in and touched her arm. 'Okay, so it was a coincidence.'

'No Simon, you don't understand. The man in this picture, my husband, is your brother.' Tears welled up.

'Now that's bloody ridiculous. I don't have a brother.'

'You do, I'll prove it.' And with that she removed some cuttings from her bag, unfolding a news cutting.

Back in England, the Raydens settled into a new home in the centre of Manchester, feeling at last they could put their own things together. The kitchen was state of the art, as they both liked to tinker with culinary experiments. Simon even tried his hand at rolling out little seaweed packages to go with their sashimi. Alison still had to ensure Simon kept the place tidy and hectored him into submission over his library of books that needed proper housing. Alison had some made-to-measure bookcases installed in oak.

The admission that day in a Japanese restaurant in the downtown business district of Hong Kong was the point when Alison had had to admit to falling for a man to replace her lost husband. Simon on the other hand had found evidence that a brother had existed. Anger followed by shock, tears followed by joy, collided. His new wife had not been deceptive but had found comfort in another relationship after her husband's death. With most new relationships it was unlikely that any contemporary romance would have some similarities with previous men. The fact it had been his brother did not matter. Many families split up when children were young. Simon's example was yet another case of a young mother forced to give up her children for adoption. Now was the time to start building their lives, but Alison was still leaving out part of the secret.

'Let's do up the Lodge'. David, her first husband and Simon's estranged brother, had used this wooden hideaway when they wanted to get away. 'I would like to go back and make it more special, as well as show off the lovely area around the Lake District. How about we take a week off?'

'Sounds a good plan to me,' Simon responded eagerly. 'I could get some walking in as I seem to have put more weight on since hanging around with you.'

'Ha, my fault is it? I don't put the food into your mouth, you big pig!' This sort of dual always ended up in the bedroom, or even on the floor, partially clothed.

Alison drove Simon to her lodge in Cumbria, set within the beautiful Lakes. Unusually, the weather was dry and sunny. The four-wheel-drive replaced her old Volvo. Simon had sold his car and now cycled everywhere. The car bumped up and down the track, the shock absorbers taking the impact. 'I've not been here since David died,' she told Simon.

'Yes, you have told me that several times.'

'So, I am just reminding you!'

'Yes, but Alison, you never told me how David died. You said it was an accident. I haven't wanted to intrude of course, but perhaps you feel comfortable enough to tell me now?'

'Darling, I know, I know, I don't want you to think I cannot confide in you.'

The car bounced down a nasty rut, throwing Simon against the door. His belt tightened just in time.

'Sorry about that, this road has always been bad but it seems to have deteriorated.'

Alison hadn't realised just how badly broken down the surface had become as she hadn't visited the lodge in a while. It has taken me the courage to do this and it is here that my personal Armageddon took place. It all seems to have happened so long ago. I hope you understand why it has been difficult for me. I know I have been evasive but I am so happy now that, well… you know how us girls are with emotions.'

Simon touched her arm sensitively. 'Okay, my treasure,' using one of his names for her.

No day had passed without Simon realising how lucky he had been in finding Alison. She was a magnet and absorbed his own emotions so overwhelmingly that he no longer saw any other women as a distraction.

'You can take your time. I'm all yours for the rest of my days,' he reassured.

Alison smiled as the route divided. A Landrover stood at the branch of the track, blocking her access. 'Oh it's Joe Baker. I haven't seen him for a while.' She touched the button and the window descended on her side. She brought the car to a halt.

'Joe, hi, how are you. Long time, eh?'

'Mrs Edwards, it is good to see you. The old Lodge has missed you.'

Joe looked at the passenger seat. Alison realised from the shocked look on his ashen face that he must be wondering who this man was, given that David had died, and Simon was very much present in the car.

'Joe, this is David's brother Simon. Doesn't he look identical?'

'Bloody hell, Mrs Edwards, for a moment I thought I was looking at a ghost there!'

Joe was old school and always called Alison 'Mrs Edwards'.

'Simon's my husband. It's a long story,' she smiled. 'David's brother married me so I am now Rayden,' she winked. Simon leaned over so he could make eye contact; he stretched his arm out to shake hands.

'Hi Joe, nice to meet you,' appearing a little confused

'Likewise,' said Joe amiably, with a big beam on his ruddy face. Joe was far from a simple man, but he was having difficulty processing this information. 'Nice to meet you, Mr Rayden, but I thought you might be Mr Edwards as well.'

'I'll come up to the farm and explain it all when I see you and Melissa. We can all have a long talk and catch up. How's Melissa though?' Alison added.

'Oh, Melissa is pregnant again.'

'Wow, that must be your third, no fourth now?'

'Oh aye, yes that is the case. The family is getting bigger, as is Melissa.'

'When is she due?'

'In eight weeks, doc reckons.'

'Look Joe, it's great seeing you again. I'll come over and see you both and we can have a drink. I have a nice bottle of wine in the back. We must get to the Lodge before dark.'

Joe put the Landrover into gear to let Alison and Simon through. He then drove back down the track Alison had driven up, as he headed to the main road.

'Joe and Melissa Baker are nice people and will always help us, I know,' she started to explain. 'His family has farmed this land for years.'

Simon realised the long-awaited explanation of David's death would have to wait. He didn't mind, and was sure that Alison would tell him in her own time and in her own way. She was such a sensitive creature and her happiness was all that he cared about.

The Lodge came into view at that moment. It was overgrown. 'Wow, I can see we have our work cut out!' Simon added, blowing his cheeks out. 'Just as well we have a bit of time on our hands. I fancy getting stuck in. At least it will make a difference from the pressures of work.'

'Yes,' Alison said almost to herself, looking out of the car window. 'Maybe a bit more run down than I thought.'

Simon grabbed the bags out of the back of the vehicle and then returned for more boxes, each crammed with provisions and bottles of wine.

'I think I had better change my shoes,' he shouted to Alison who was now inside the wooden building.

'What's that, darling?'

'I said my shoes…'

He stopped in midsentence and added, 'Wow, that's a great fireplace,' he said, admiring an old stone chimney that took up the centre of the house.

'Have we any logs?'

'Yes, I picked up a bag of logs from the garage but I fear they might be too damp. Please be a dear and get them for me so we can dry them,' she said.

'Yes boss, no problem,' and he went back to the car.

Simon dumped the logs, now devoid of packaging, and spread them out around the stone fireplace. He heard Alison rummaging around in the kitchen.

'Oh, and can you turn the gas on? It's in a box outside the kitchen window.'

'Anything else while I'm at it?' he shouted with mock irritation. There was no answer. He found a box at the side of the lodge with rusty, torn hinges. Considering rules on safety these days, he wasn't sure this was ideal, but he found that the bottle inside the box was dry and covered with a mild patina of rust. The top had a regulator and a switch. He flicked this and shouted back at Alison. 'Is it working?'

'Yes, the gas is working. Fancy a cuppa?'

'Sounds great, I'm going to explore a bit.'

'Don't be long then, sweetheart.' She heard no reply. 'Then don't be long,' she repeated but he had left.

Simon walked around the Lodge. Dense bushes had grown up the sides of the log cabin, briar penetrating the bush. Ivy had taken hold, with little suckers marking the wooden fascia. He made a mental note to clear this back. As he reached the back of the lodge, he saw a large shed and wondered if there were any tools inside to do the job. The door was open. One side was a little lower where one hinge drooped. He noticed it needed a good paint. While this was happening, Simon was unaware of the dark shadow standing under the tree nearby. It was long and had an aura...

Alison was soon in her element. The water was on the stove and heating up for tea. She used bottled water for drinks, as the tap water was somewhat brown due to disuse. She opened the cupboard doors, searching for mugs. The familiar damp smell of poorly ventilated space hit her. 'Another job' she told herself.

An old weathered newspaper lay dry and crinkled in one corner. The local gazette had reported the news.

'Dear, dear Lodge' she said, 'I'm sorry I have not been back to visit you. We had such good times here. Dear David did not deserve to die. I must do all I can to protect my new man...'

Simon pushed the door open. Compressed, musty earth carpeted the shed's floor. Various rusty implements were hanging by orange twine from wooden beams. A bench stood in front of him, complete with sturdy vice. 'That's good,' he told himself. 'I really need to get back to DIY; it has been a long time.' There was a dim light in the shed. A sudden brightness came and went, puzzling him. It was as if someone had been there and now was not. His foot hit the jerry can with a clang. It was a dark green metal can, and as he lifted it, it seemed half full. He felt some rust on the handle and at the same time saw a light switch. He flicked the switch and dim light appeared from a 60-watt bulb. He noted it was the old fashioned type rather than the newer low emission ones which saved energy. He looked down at the can again and stroked the handle. No, this was not rust, this looked like dry blood! It was pretty thick...

She flicked the newspaper over and came to page 2. Alison still found this a hard-to-read piece, written about her husband. She hated the dispassionate description, no doubt written by a lowly journalist.

> Local man, David Edwards, 52 years of age, lost his life when his chainsaw severed an artery in his leg. David was married to Alison. They had no children. They were well known to locals and David was popular. They kept a log cabin at Renshaw Creek in the Lake District. David was pronounced dead on arrival...

The kettle seemed to boil slowly, but finally Alison heard the whistle. 'Won't be long, my honey bunch,' she said to herself, 'And we can have that nice cuppa. Now where are those chocolate biscuits Simon likes? Mind you, better be careful as that waist of his has crept up...'

Simon had seen enough blood in his career as a podiatric surgeon to know this was not normal. The colour had splashed liberally down the can. He looked around and saw a chainsaw. 'Ah, I guess this is why the petrol can is here as it would have to be petrol driven.' He opened the polyethene fuel tank. Having unscrewed the cap it dangled connected to a chain. Looking inside he sniffed. The light caught the colour of the chainsaw. The words on the side appeared obscured by more blood. The cruel chain itself was otherwise clean.

He was startled by a voice and turned for the source. 'I cleaned most of that up after the accident.'

'Joe, Christ almighty you startled me. Don't go creeping up on people. My heart is not young anymore.' He told Joe off, smiling with relief.

'Thought I had better come back. Your missus, she is a goodun, helped me and Melissa back then when the taxman tried to take my farm. I decided to come back as this place needs some work and thought you might like some dry wood.'

'Yes, you can say that again,' nodding in agreement. 'She bought some logs from the garage but I doubt they will be dry before tomorrow. Why they don't store them somewhere dry I'll never know.'

'I've got a dry tree in the back of the truck. I cut it down last year so it will be reasonably seasoned. Reckoned Mrs Ed— I mean Rayden, could do with the wood so I brought it up. Right, we just need to cut it up a bit more and then you can use it tonight.'

Joe hauled the tree out of his Landrover with ease. He was a big man with bulging muscles.

'Bring that chainsaw over. I checked it over and it's been tested and ready to go,' he announced confidently.

'You pour the fuel mix in while I get my axe,' Joe said, moving back to his vehicle.

The shadow moved fluidly, hovering, and came into the light. The aura brightened, increasing to a blinding light. A silvery figure matched the height of the dark shadow. The two appeared as coloured chess pieces bound together.

'All done,' said Simon.

'Right, fire it up,' said Joe...

Alison heard the first turn of the motor and froze! It took her what seemed like ages to comprehend the noise and where it had come from. Her face went white with dread...

The image in white disappeared and became black. Death looked on...

'Nooooo...' Alison screamed.

She raced out of the kitchen and down the steps three at a time, nearly stumbling. The noise was now well established as the spark plug did its job. The motor roared into life… The chain moved around, the cruel teeth set to do business with the wood it was about to engage. Most people used protection and thick reinforced leggings, but Joe and Simon only had on regular clothing, although Joe was wearing work boots. A flash of white appeared again, dulling Death's image, but nothing could stop the bang as the chainsaw whirred out of control. The man holding the chainsaw fell dead instantly, the wound mortal, from which no one could survive.

Two weeks later, Alison stood at the graveside dressed in black. The veil hid her blotchy, tear-streaked face as the vicar read the service. The grave, freshly dug, was surrounded by Joe's family. Melissa stood, heavily pregnant. The youngest held her hand tightly. Others attended, but Alison was oblivious to them. The coffin lowered. Melissa gave a loud cry of anguish. Simon gripped Alison's hand.

EPILOGUE

Death was Sycastra and Sycastra was death. One side gave off blinding light so that an obsidian colour almost obscured the left-hand side. No one could see either image, so well were they contrasted. Life fought death and good fought evil. 'So, why did you save him?' one voice spoke to no one in particular, not that anyone could hear.

The other voice said, 'Because he was not ready and the other one was.'

The enquiry published findings revealing a recent service and nothing wrong with the chainsaw. Joe's autopsy revealed he had overwhelming cancer.

Author's note

Hong Kong left British control in 1997 as a lease ended with China. It was not until 2010 I was able to visit when it was clear the vestiges of British rule had started to subside. Ten years later, the changes were more visible when I took the love of my own life to South East Asia. China had imposed draconian powers, snuffing out all the ideals of democracy.

Fascinated by the food and markets as I travelled around this compact series of islands, I wanted to use some of my travel log as background to the love affair complicated by that rare opportunity of a new contract called marriage.

As far as Tarot cards are concerned, death represents the shedding required to continue progressing along one's path. We learn that while there is a feeling of grief present alongside that fear of the unknown, there's a new beginning on the other side if you can stick it out.

My story is of course fiction and Sycastra a figment of my imagination, taken from the 14th-century concepts of the Grim Reaper, scything life from the ground. We of course met *him* – or is it *her*, or *it* – in 'Sticky Contract'. However, Sycastra is more complicated. He seeks out death but with a strange conscience merged between male and female minds, hence the white aura representing good instead of evil, right and wrong, justice and redemption. Sycastra will identify the disease and terminate life. For without 'it' we would all become the living dead.

ACKNOWLEDGMENTS

Whether writing fact or fiction, authors are influenced by events, people and the environment.

Fatal Contracts emerged from many stories which could never have reached the page without people and places. The characters of course are fictional but we are all drawn to the real world in order sketch out a story that resonates with life. I decided to provide authors notes for each story so the reader could discern fact from fiction. There are a number of people I must credit for their kind assistance in making this book better for their critique. As always any errors are my own.

Anne-Marie my copy editor. Sid Gibson provided me with his insight into my writing style and offered some great tips. Roy Jones for his input into '*Brodie's Deception*' from which I benefitted from his weight of historical knowledge. Richard Lishman, who advised me on the financial sector in '*The Piscarro Contract*'.

Rachel Curran who contributed to my chapter on '*A strange Affair*'. I would also like to thank Derek Pearson who looked over the original scribblings with his own author's eye and provided the type of critique all new authors must have when embarking on fictional writing.

As always I am truly grateful to my cover designer Petya Tsankova who always gives one hundred and ten percent to my projects and is more than just a cover creator. Lastly, to my wife Jill, who is tolerant of the many hours I spend hiding away but, she happens to be brilliant at critique and great proof reader and quick to challenge – her word is final so thank you for making me better than I really am.

David R Tollafield

ABOUT THE AUTHOR

Born in Hitchin Hertfordshire in 1956 David was a former podiatric surgeon and lecturer. He qualified from London Foot Hospital, University College Hospital in 1978.

He worked in the British National Health Service as well as working in the independent sector as a consultant for 30 years, retiring in 2018 to write full time.

He lives with his wife Jill in the West Country. His website www.consultingfootpain allows him to stay in touch with a wide range of readers and when not writing he publishes health articles.

Fatal Contracts is his first adult fiction book.

He is keen on amateur dramatics, Nordic walking, public speaking, travelling and researching military history.

David R Tollafield

Other books by the author

NON FICTION

Myths, Facts & Fables. A Podiatrist's Reflection on
Foot Health

Podiatrist on a Mission. *The Genesis of a New
Profession*

Selling Foot Health as Podiatry

Projecting Your Image. *Conference to Village Halls*

PowerPoint is More than a Slide Program

Bunion Hallux Valgus. *Behind the Scenes.*

Morton's Neuroma. *Podiatrist Turned Patient: My
Own Journey*

With Linda Merriman
Clinical Skills in Treating the Foot
Assessment of the Lower Limb

Printed in Great Britain
by Amazon